걷는 독서

READING WHILE WALKING ALONG

걷는 독서

READING WHILE WALKING ALONG

박노해

PARK NOHAE

느린걸음

마음아 천천히
천천히 걸어라.
내 영혼이 길을 잃지 않도록.

Ah, heart, slowly,
slowly, walk.
Lest my soul lose its way.

6

서문

돌아보니 그랬다. 나는 늘 길 찾는 사람이었다. 길을 걷는 사람이었고 '걷는 독서'를 하는 이였다.

　어린 날 마을 언덕길이나 바닷가 방죽에서 풀 뜯는 소의 고삐를 쥐고 책을 읽었고, 학교가 끝나면 진달래꽃 조팝꽃 산수국꽃 핀 산길을 걸으며 책을 읽었다. 벚꽃잎이 하르르 하르르 날리는 길을 걸으며, 푸르게 일렁이는 보리밭 사이를 걸으며, 가을바람에 물든 잎이 지는 길을 걸으며, 붉은 동백꽃이 떨어진 흰 눈길을 걸으며 '걷는 독서'를 했다. 오래된 책 향기에 계절의 향기가 스미고, 바람의 속삭임과 안개의 술렁임과 새의 노래가 흐르고, 여명의 희푸른 빛이 오고 붉은 노을이 물들면, 책 속의 활자와 길의 풍경들 사이로 어떤 전언傳言이 들려오곤 했다. '걷는 독서'를 할 때면 나는 두 세상 사이의 유랑자로 또 다른 세계를 걸어가고 있었다.

　유년의 가난과 고독과 슬픔의 허기로 먹어 치운 책들이 내 안에서 푸른 나무로 자라났고, 청년이 되어 군사독재 시대의 한가운데로 나는 불화

살처럼 내달렸다. 그리하여 내게 주어진 가장 가혹한 형벌은 걷지 못하는 것이었다.

나는 무기수가 되어 한 평짜리 어둑한 감옥 독방에 던져졌다. 한 걸음 두 걸음 반이면 눈앞에 쇠창살, 돌아서 한 걸음 두 걸음 반이면 코앞에 벽이었다. 그 작은 감옥 독방에서도 '걷는 독서'를 계속했다. 비록 세상 맨 밑바닥 끝자리에 놓인 두 걸음 반짜리 길의 반복이었으나 '걷는 독서'를 하는 내 정신의 공간은 그 어떤 탐험가나 정복자보다 광활했다. 수많은 역사 시대와 사건 현장과 별들, 저 별들 사이를 걸어 다녔다. 철저히 고립되고 감시받는 감옥 독방의 그 짧고도 기나긴 길에서 아, 나는 얼마나 많은 인물과 사상을 마주하고 얼마나 깊은 시간과 차원의 신비를 여행했던가.

자유의 몸이 되고 국경 너머 눈물 흐르는 지구의 골목길에서도 나의 '걷는 독서'는 계속되었다. 폭음이 울리는 격렬한 일정 사이로 햇살이 좋은 날이면 '걷는 독서'로 다친 마음을 다잡곤 했다. 만년설산 고원과 불타는 사막과 알 자지라 평원과 칼데라와 광야의 '걷는 독서'는 내 두 발로 입맞춤

하는 그 땅에 대한 의례와도 같았다. '걷는 독서'는 나의 일과이자 나의 기도이고 내 창조의 원천이었다. 나는 그렇게 길 위의 '걷는 독서'로 단련되어왔다. 내 인생의 풍경을 단 한 장에 새긴다면 '걷는 독서'를 하는 모습이 아닐까 생각하기도 한다.

돌아보니 그랬다. 가난과 노동과 고난으로 점철된 내 인생길에서 그래도 나를 키우고 나를 지키고 나를 밀어 올린 것은 '걷는 독서'였다. 어쩌면 모든 것을 빼앗긴 내 인생에서 그 누구도 빼앗지 못한 나만의 자유였고 나만의 향연이었다.

어느덧 내 생의 날들에 가을이 오고 흰 여백의 인생 노트도 점점 얇아지고 있다. 만년필에 담아 쓰는 잉크는 갈수록 피처럼 진해지기만 해서, 아껴 써야만 하는 남은 생의 백지를 묵연히 바라본다.

그리하여 날마다 계속되는 나의 반성은 이것이다. 나는 너무 많이 읽고 너무 많이 쓰고 있는 것은 아닌가. 내가 일생 동안 거듭 읽고 다시 읽어온 건 가장 오래 전승된 짧은 말씀들이 아닌가. 그것들은 죽간에 붓으로 쓰거나 양피지에 깃촉으로 쓰거나 돌에 새겨진 말 중의 말, 글 중의 글들이 아닌가. '적게 말하여라. 많은 것을 적은 말로 하여라.' 그래서 나는, 단호한 원칙과 각오로 내 모든 글을 만년필로 종이에 꾹꾹 눌러쓰고 있지만, 육필 원고가 키 높이를 넘어갈 때면 이마저 세상에 소음과 잡음을 더하는 것이 아닌가 반성을 한다.

그럴 때면 책상 위에 놓인 담뱃갑 크기의 작고 얇은 벼루를 꺼내 오래오래 먹을 갈아 붓으로 글을 쓰곤 한다. 수백 년 세월을 걸어와 나에게 주어진 이 벼루의 주인은 누구였을까. 말을 타고 초원과 사막을 달리다 하많은 생각과 문장들이 자신을 못살게 할 때면 벼루에 먹을 갈아 귀한 죽간이나 종이에 심사숙고한 단 한 줄을 썼으리라. 그 사유의 밀도, 말의 함축, 폭발할 듯 응축된 한 문장. 이 작고 오래된 벼루는 나에게 더 깊이 생각하고 더 적게 쓰라고, 더 충실히 살아내고 더 많이 침묵하라고, 나를 불살라 사랑한 것만을 쓰라고, 검고 깊은 눈동자로 나를 응시하고 있는 것이다.

만일 내가 한 달에 몇 병씩 쓰는 잉크 병에 내 붉은 피를 담아 쓴다면, 그러면 난 어떻게 쓸까.

더 적게 쓰고 더 짧게 쓸 것이 아닌가. 한 자 한 자 목숨 걸고 살아낸 것만을 쓰고 최후의 유언처럼 심혈을 기울여 쓸 것이 아닌가. 나는 그런 글만을 써야 한다고 몸부림쳐왔다.

우린 지금 너무 많이 읽고 너무 많이 알고 너무 많이 경험하고 있다. 잠시도 내면의 느낌에 머물지 못하고 깊은 침묵과 고독을 견디지 못하고, 끊임없이 찾아다니고 찍어 올리고 나를 알리고 얼굴도 모르는 이들의 인정을 구하고 있다. 그리하여 책을 읽는 것조차 경쟁이 되고 과시와 장식의 독서가 되고 말았다. 독서가 도구화될 때, 그것은 거룩한 책의 약탈이다. 내가 책 속의 지식을 약탈하는 듯하지만 그 지식이 나의 생을 약탈하고 있다.

진정한 독서란 지식을 축적하는 '자기 강화'의 독서가 아닌 진리의 불길에 나를 살라내는 '자기 소멸'의 독서다. 책을 '읽었다'와 책을 '읽어버렸다'의 엄청난 차이를 알 것이다. 읽어버리는 순간, 어떤 숨결이 일었고, 어떤 불꽃이 피었고, 저 영원의 빛에 감광되어 버렸고 그로부터 내 안의 무언가 결정적으로 살라지고 비워지고 만 것이다. 그 소멸의 자리만큼이 진정한 나를 마주하고 새로운 삶을 잉태하는 하나의 성소인 것이다.

　나는 보았다. 아니, 보아버리고 말았다. 나는 만났다. 아니, 만나버리고 말았다. 나는 읽었다. 아니, 읽어버리고 말았다. 그 순간 나는 이제까지의 나를 '버리고' 그 진리 앞에 응답해야 한다. 책으로의 도피나 마취가 아닌 온 삶으로 읽고, 읽어버린 것을 살아내야만 한다. 독서의 완성은 삶이기에. 그리하여 우리 모두는 저마다 한 권의 책을 써나가는 사람이다. 삶이라는 단 한 권의 책을.

　이 책은 지난 30여 년 동안 날마다 계속해온 나의 '걷는 독서' 길에서 번쩍, 불꽃이 일면 발걸음을 멈추고 수첩에 새겨온 '한 생각'이다. 눈물로 쓴 일기장이고 간절한 기도문이며 내 삶의 고백록이자 나직한 부르짖음이기도 하다. 그리고 그리운 그대에게 보내는 두꺼운 편지다. 저 먼 사막 끝 마을에서 흰 설원에 이르기까지, 그곳의 가슴 시린 나의 풍경을 찍은 사진엽서 한 장에 돌에 새기듯

썼으나 부치지 못하고 차곡차곡 담아온 편지다.

지금 세계에 검은 그림자가 드리우고 사람과 사람 사이에 장벽이 세워지고 있다. 그러나 인간은 걷는 존재이고 만남의 존재이고 읽는 존재이다. 앞이 보이지 않는 불안하고 삭막한 이 시대에, 부디 아프지 말고 다치지 말고 사라지지 말자고 이제 와 내 품속의 편지를 띄워 보낸다. 이 『걷는 독서』가 그대 안에 있는 하많은 생각과 지식들을 '목적의 단 한 줄'로 꿰어내는 삶의 화두가 되고 창조의 영감이 되고 어려운 날의 도약대가 되기를.

어디서든 어디서라도 나만의 길을 걸으며 '걷는 독서'를 멈추지 말자. 간절한 마음으로 읽을 때, 사랑, 사랑의 불로 읽어버릴 때, 『걷는 독서』는 나를 키우고 나를 지키고 나를 밀어 올리는 신비한 그 힘을 그대 자신으로부터 길어내 줄테니. '걷는 독서'를 하는 순간, 그대는 이미 저 영원의 빛으로 이어진 두 세상 사이를 걸어가고 있으니.

2021년 6월
박노해

Preface

Looking back, it was always so. I have always been someone in search of a path. I was someone walking along a path, someone "reading while walking along."

In my youth, I used to read a book while holding the bridle of a cow grazing on the village hillside or the beach's bank, and after school, I would be "reading while walking along" mountain paths bright with azalea flowers, bridal wreath flowers, hydrangea flowers. Walking along paths as cherry blossom petals went drifting gently, walking between rolling green barley fields, walking along paths where colored leaves were falling in the autumn breeze, and walking along white snowy paths where red camellia flowers had fallen, I would be "reading while walking along." When the scent of the season mingled with the fragrance of an old book, while the whisper of the wind, the stirring of the mist, and the songs of the birds flowed by, the pale gray light of dawn would come and red sunsets would glow, I would hear messages emerging between the words printed in the book and the scenery along the road. When I was "reading while walking along," I went walking through another world as a wanderer between two worlds.

The books I devoured with the hunger of childhood poverty, solitude and sorrow grew up into green trees within me, and once I was a young man, I sped like a blazing arrow into the midst of the era of military dictatorship. So the harshest punishment I've ever been given was not being able to walk.

I became a prisoner with a life sentence and was thrown into a gloomy prison cell of barely three square yards. One, two and a half steps and the iron bars were in front of me, one, two and a half steps and the wall was in front of me. Yet even in that tiny prison cell, I continued "reading while walking along." Although it was merely a repetition of a two-and-a-half-step path at the lowest point of the world, the space of my mind as I went "reading while walking along" was wider than any explorer or conqueror. I walked among numerous historical periods, places of events and stars, among the stars. Along that short yet long road of the prison cell, completely isolated and monitored, ah, how many people and thoughts I encountered, what deep time and mysteries of dimensions I traveled through.

Once I was free, my "reading while walking along" continued along the tearful alleys of the world, beyond all borders. On sunny days between violent moments echoing with explosions, I used to hold my wounded heart as I went "reading while walking along." In highlands with snow-capped peaks, burning deserts, the Al Jazeera Plain, caldera and wildernesses, "reading while walking along" was like a ritual for the land kissed by my own two feet. "Reading while walking along" was my daily routine, my prayer and the source of my creation. Thus I have been disciplined by "reading while walking along." I rather think that if I have to inscribe the scenery of my life on a single page, it would show me "reading while walking along."

Looking back, it was always so. Along my life's path marked by poverty, labor and hardship, it was "reading while walking along" that raised me, protected me, and pushed me upward. Even if I am robbed to everything, it was the one freedom and the one banquet that no one could steal from my life.

Autumn has come in the days of my life, my life note with white margins is growing thinner and thinner. The ink in my fountain pen grows ever thicker like blood, as I gaze silently at the blank pages of the rest of my life that I have to use sparingly.

So this is my daily reflection. Maybe I'm reading too much and writing too much. What I have read and reread, over and over again, in my life are the short words that have been handed down longest, words chosen from among the words written with a brush on bamboo slips or a quill on parchment sheets, carved in stone, writings chosen from among writings, "Say little. Say much with few words." So while I note down all my writings using a fountain pen with firm principle and determination, when my manuscript rises higher than myself, I wonder if it is not simply adding to the noise and uproar of the world.

At such times, I take the small, thin inkstone, the size of a pack of cigarettes, that is lying on my desk, grind ink for a very long time, and write with a brush. Who was the first owner of this inkstone that was given to me after travelling through hundreds of years? Maybe after many thoughts and sentences had made him miserable while he sped on horseback over meadows and deserts, he would have ground ink on this inkstone then written a single thoughtful line on bamboo or paper. A single phrase where the density of the thought and the implications of the words were so condensed they seemed about to explode. This little old inkstone stares at me with deep, black eyes, telling me to think more deeply and write less, to live more faithfully and observe more silence, to write only what I have loved, setting myself alight.

If I poured my own red blood into the ink bottles of which I use several a month, then how would I write? Surely, I would write less, shorter, would write one word, one word only what I have risked my life for, put my whole life into writing, like a last will. I have been struggling, telling myself that I should write only that kind of writing.

Nowadays we read too much, know too much, experience too much. We can't stay still with our inner feelings for a moment, can't stand deep silence and solitude, we are constantly roaming around, uploading selfies, making ourselves known, seeking recognition from those who don't even know our face. Thus, even reading books has become competitive and reading is done for ostentation and decoration. When reading becomes utilitarian it is the plundering of holy books. It's as if I am plundering the knowledge in the book, but that knowledge is plundering my life.

True reading is not "self-enhancing" reading that accumulates knowledge, but a reading of "self-obliteration" that burns us up by the flames of truth. You can see the huge difference between 'reading' a book and 'fully reading' a book. When I read fully, a breath arises, a breeze blows, a flame kindles, I am exposed to a light of eternity, and by it something in me is decisively burnt, emptied away. Insofar as it is a place of obliteration it is a sanctuary where I face the true me and conceive a new life.

I saw. No, I fully saw. I met. No, I fully met. I read. No, I fully read. At that moment I must finally cast off myself and respond to the truth. Reading with my whole life, not books as escape or anesthesia, I have to live what I have fully read, for the perfection of reading is life. Thus we each are an individual engaged in writing a book. Just one book, called Life.

This book is "a thought" that has been engraved in my notebook when a flame arises, flashing on my path after I stop walking as I go "reading while walking along," something which has continued every day for the past thirty years. It is a diary written in tears, an earnest prayer, a confession of my life, and a low cry. And it's a thick letter addressed to you, whom I miss. From that village at the far end of a desert to a white snow field, an accumulated pile of letters written as though carved on stone on postcards of photos I took of heartbreaking views of that place, that I could not mail.

Now there are black shadows cast over the world and barriers rise between people. But humans are walking beings, meeting beings, and reading beings. In this unstable and desolate era where we cannot see what lies ahead, I am sending you a letter from my heart now urging us not to fall sick, not to be wounded, not to disappear. May this *Reading While Walking Along* become a topic of life linking together many thoughts and knowledge within you into a "single line of purpose," an inspiration for creation, and a springboard on difficult days.

Let's never stop "reading while walking along" anywhere, at any point, as we each walk along our own path. When you read with an earnest heart, read fully with love, a fire of love, *Reading While Walking Along* will sustain you, protect you, and bring out the mysterious power that pushes you up from yourself. As you go "reading while walking along," you are already walking between two worlds leading to that eternal light.

June, 2021
Park Nohae

꽃은 달려가지 않는다.

Flowers never hurry.

자신감 갖기가 아닌
자신이 되기.

Becoming a self
does not mean
having self-confidence.

앞이 보이지 않는 것은
어둠이 깊어서가 아니다.
너무 현란한 빛에
눈이 멀어서이다.

If we cannot see what lies ahead,
it is not because the darkness
has grown deeper.
Our eyes have been blinded
by too bright a light.

너와 나, 이 만남을 위해
우리는 오랜 시간 서로를 향해
마주 걸어오고 있었다.

For this encounter, you and I
have been walking toward each other
for a very long time.

내가 가장 상처받는 지점이
내가 가장 욕망하는 지점이다.

The point where I am most wounded
is the point where I crave most.

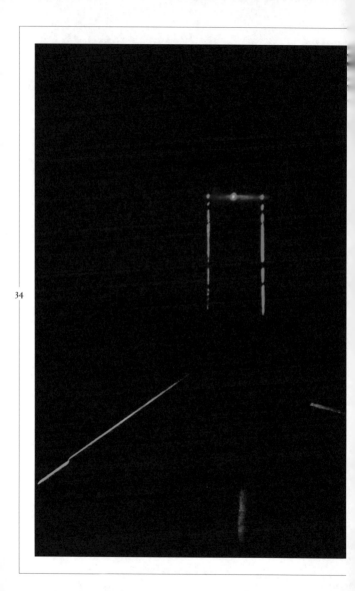

삶은 짧아도 영원을 사는 것.
영원이란 '끝도 없이'가 아니라
'지금 완전히' 사는 것이다.

No matter how short,
life is a matter of living eternity.
Eternity is not a matter of
'having no end,' but of 'living fully now.'

일을 사랑하지 말고
사랑이 일하게 하라.

Do not love work,
make love work.

나는 이 지상에
비밀히 던져진 씨앗 하나.
아무도 모른다.
내 안에서 무엇이 피어날지.

I am a seed sown
secretly here on earth.
Nobody knows
what will blossom within me.

행복은 그림자 같은 것.
잡으러 뛰어가면 달아나고
문득 돌아보면 가만히
나를 따라오는 것.

Happiness is like my shadow.
If I run trying to catch it, it flees
and if I suddenly look back,
it is quietly following me.

차별은 없애고
차이는 살리고.

Abolish discrimination,
let difference live.

내가 소유한 것들이
나를 소유하게 하지 말며
내가 올라선 자리가
나를 붙박게 하지 말기를.

May the things that
I own not own me,
may the place I rise up to
not hold me fixed.

막막한 날도 있어야 하리.
떨리는 날도 있어야 하리.
그래, 꽃피는 날이 오리니.

There have to be dreary days.
There have to be trembling days.
Right, and then days will come
when flowers bloom.

1월은 새로 시작하는 달.
새로와진 얼굴로 인사를 하고
새로운 마음으로 길을 나서는 달.

January, a month for new beginnings.
A month for greeting
each other with new faces,
for setting out with new hearts.

알려지지 않았다고
존재하지 않는 것은 아니다.
드러나지 않는다고
위대하지 않은 것은 아니다.

Saying I have not been recognized
does not mean I do not exist.
Saying I have not been noticed
does not mean I am not great.

힘으로 열 수 없는 문이 하나 있다.
사람의 마음 문이다.
힘으로 그를 꺾을 수는 있어도
힘으로 마음을 얻을 수는 없다.

There is a door
that cannot be forced open.
The door of a human heart.
Though force may bend and break it,
a heart can never be gained by force.

바라본다는 것은 바라며 본다는 것.
사람은 그가 바라보는 대로 되어간다.

Looking is hoping.
As we hope and look, so we become.

쓰는 것이 삶이 되게 하지 마라.
절실한 삶이 써 나가게 하라.

Don't let writing become your life.
Let you fervent life issue in writing.

어둠 속을 떨며 걸어온 인생은 알리라.
아침에 눈을 뜨면 눈부신 세상이 있고
나에게 또 하루가 주어졌다는 게
얼마나 큰 경이인지.

The life that comes shaking off
darkness teaches us.
When morning comes after walking
trembling through the darkness
I sense how wonderful it is that
such another day has dawned.

겨울을 뚫고 왔다.
우리는 봄의 전위.
이 외로운 겨울 산천에
봄불 내주고 쓰러지기 위해
붉게 왔다.
내 등 뒤에 꽃피어 오는
너를 위하여.

We pierced
our way through winter.
We are spring's avant-garde.
We came to collapse,
blazing red, bringing spring fire
to this lonely winter landscape.
For you who are coming
blossoming behind me.

자기밖에 모르는 삶은 흔한 비극이다.
자기마저 모르는 삶은 더한 비극이다.

A life aware only of itself
is a common tragedy.
A life unaware even of itself
is a greater tragedy.

똑똑한 사람은 알맞게 옳은 말을 하고
지혜로운 사람은 때맞춰 침묵할 줄 안다.

A clever person speaks
the right words at the right time,
a wise person knows
when it's time to be silent.

우리 인생은 '별 일', 별의 일이다.
우주적 생의 일, 하늘의 일이다.
우리 모두는 '별 볼 일' 있는 생이다.

Our life is star-blessed, not star-crossed,
a cosmic life, a heavenly life.
Each of our lives is star-blessed.

봄이 오면 얼음 박힌 내 몸에
간질간질 새싹이 터오르고
금방 꽃이 필 것만 같아서.

When spring comes,
my icebound body
itches to put out fresh buds
and seems about to blossom.

사랑을 구하려고 두리번거리지 않았지.
사랑으로 살다 보니 사랑이 찾아왔지.

I have never gazed around
intent on gaining love.
As I lived a loving life love came calling.

젊음은 위험하다.
세상을 파괴하기 때문이 아니라
세상을 창조하기 때문이다.

Youth is dangerous.
Not because it destroys the world
but because it creates the world.

실패 앞에 정직하게 성찰하게 하소서.
지금의 실패가 오히려 나의 길을 찾아가는
하나의 이정표임을 잊지 않게 하소서.

May I reflect seriously when faced with failure.
May I never forget that present failure
is a signpost enabling me to find my path.

여행은 떠나는 것이 아니라
찾아옴을 향해 걷는 것이다.

A journey is not a matter of departing,
it's walking toward a visit.

78

생각의 속도보다 중요한 것은
생각의 차원이고
생각의 방향이다.

More important than
the speed of a thought
is its level
and direction.

사람은 영물이라서
어떤 마음으로 하는지 다 안다.
사람이 하늘이다.
사람이 영물이다.

Since humans are spiritual beings
we know with what heart each acts.
Humans are Heaven.
Humans are spiritual beings.

머리 굴리지 말고
욕심 세우지 말고
겉멋 부리지 말고
단순하게 그냥 가기.
본질로만 승부하기.

Not playing tricks,
not being greedy,
not dressing up,
advancing simply.
Making do with
what you are.

많은 만남보다 속 깊은 만남을.

Profound encounters rather than
multiple encounters.

겨울은 위로부터 으슬으슬 내려왔지만
봄은 아래로부터 으쓱으쓱 밀어옵니다.
겨울은 얇은 자에게 먼저 몰아쳐 왔지만
봄은 많이 떨고 견딘 자에게 먼저 옵니다.

Winter came dropping shivering from above,
but spring rises proudly from below.
Winter first came raging to skinny people,
but spring comes first to those
who shiver and endure.

내가 희망을 만드는 것이 아니라
희망이 나를 만들어간다.

I do not make hope,
hope makes me in passing.

중단하지 않는 한 실패가 아니다.

So long as I did not come to a halt,
nothing is failure.

세상에는 두 부류의 사람이 있다.
힘을 사랑하는 자와
사랑의 힘을 가진 자.

There are two kinds of people
in the world.
Those who love power and
those who have the power of love.

낡은 만년필에
희망을 장전하고
절망을 향해 쓴다.

Filling my old fountain pen
with hope
I write against despair.

얼마나 떨었기에 연두 싹이 솟구치나.
얼마나 얼었기에 붉은 불로 타오르나.

How much did a green shoot shudder
before emerging?
How much did it freeze
before arising as a crimson flame?

우리는 태양을 직접 바라볼 수 없다.
태양이 기르고 빛내는 것으로만 확인될 뿐.
참으로 큰 사랑은 보이지 않는다.

We cannot look directly at the sun.
The sun is known by giving growth and light.
Truly great love cannot be seen.

인간 세상의 그 어떤 위대한 일도
따뜻한 밥 한 그릇에서 시작된다.

Every great task in life
begins with a hot bowl of rice.

살아있는 모든 이는
죽은 자를 딛고 서 있다.

All who live
walk and stand on the dead.

빛과 어둠에는 총량이 있듯이
기쁨에도 슬픔에도 총량이 있다.
행운에도 불행에도 총량이 있다.

Just as light and darkness have volume,
so too joy and sorrow have volume.
Happiness and unhappiness too
have volume.

울지마.
사랑한 만큼
슬픈 거니까.

Don't cry.
Your degree of sorrow
matches that of your love.

내가 진정 살아야 할 삶이 있건만
아직도 그 삶을 살지 못하여
이렇게 사무치는 마음인가.

Is my heart pierced thus
because there is a life
I really should live
but so far I could not live it?

말하는 것은 어느새 쉽게 배워버린다.
먼저 침묵하는 법을 배워야 한다.

Learning how to speak is suddenly easy.
First you have to learn how to be silent.

아이들은 우리 몸을 거쳐왔을 뿐.
아이들은 우리가 가볼 수 없는
아득한 미래를 살고 있는 것을.
그저 뜨거운 믿음으로,
애타는 사랑으로, 이 지상에
잠시 동행하는 기쁨을 허락하기를.

Children simply came by
way of our bodies.
They live the distant future
that we cannot experience,
simply allowing us the joy
of briefly accompanying them,
with warm trust,
burning love, in this world.

이 소란한 세계의 한 구석에
내 영혼이 오롯이 앉을 수 있는
오래되고 아늑한 의자 하나.
잠깐, 생각에 잠기는 그 순간
하나의 세계가 탄생하는 자리.

In one corner of this noisy world
an old, cozy chair
where my soul can sit properly.
A place where,
after a moment's thought,
a world is born.

3월에는 수고했습니다 인사를 한다.
풀꽃에게도 그대에게도.
힘겨움 속에서 새롭게 태어나느라.

In March our greeting is:
You've worked hard.
To flowering plants, and you as well,
all being laboriously born anew.

아무 말도 하지 않아도
그냥 바라만 보아도 좋은 사람.
이 지구에 함께 있어주는 것만으로
내가 사는 힘이 되는 그런 이가 있다.

A good person who simply looks,
even without saying a word.
There are people who give me
strength to go on living
simply by being with me on this Earth.

경험은 소유하고 쌓아가는 것이 아니다.
체험 속에 나를 소멸해가는 것이다.

Experience is not something
owned and accumulated.
Inside experience is what will extinguish me.

자기만의 스타일을 찾는 것은
고유한 나 자신을 찾는 것과 같다.

Looking for one's own special style
is the same as looking
for my unique self.

제일 좋아하는 열 개의 단어를 적어보라.
제일 경멸하는 열 개의 단어를 적어보라.
그러면 내가 누구인지 드러날 것이다.

Write down your favorite ten words.
Write down the ten words you most despise.
Then you'll see clearly who you are.

말씀은 가만가만.
걸음은 나직나직.
마음은 한들한들.

Word, gently, gently.
Steps, softly, softly.
The heart, trembling, trembling.

별이 자신을 불태우며 빛나듯
사랑은 자신을 다 사르는 것.

Just as a star shines
as it burns itself up,
love burns and consumes itself.

마음씨는 마음의 씨앗.
지금의 마음가짐이 씨앗이 되어
그 모든 결실을 뒤바꾼다.

The heart is the seed of the heart.
Your current disposition
becomes a seed
that makes all the difference.

혼자면 너무 외롭고
둘이면 불안하지만
시작은 작아도 셋이면 충분하다.

Too lonely alone, uncertain if two,
but even with small beginnings
three is ample.

비울수록 새 힘이 차오른다.

The more you empty out,
the more strength comes rising.

한 사회가 무너지기 전에
먼저 사람이 무너지고
한 사회가 바로 서기 전에
먼저 사람이 일어선다.

Before a society falls
first people fall,
and before a society is set upright
first people rise up.

정치의 본질은
'약한 자 힘주고
강한 자 바르게'.

The essence of politics:
Giving power to the weak,
setting the powerful straight.

나만을 위한 나일 때
아 나는 얼마나 작으냐.

When I exist only for myself,
alas, how small I am.

관심에는 총량이 있다.
우선순위를 바로 하기.
단념할 것을 단념하기.

Interest has limits.
Establishing priorities.
Giving up
what is to be given up.

그냥 걸어라.
첫걸음마 하는 아이처럼
내 영혼이 부르는 길을
그냥 걸어라.

Just start walking.
Like a baby taking its first steps.
Just start walking
along the path my soul calls for.

봄은 볼 게 많아서 봄.
아직 보이지 않는 것을 보는 봄.
마음의 눈을 뜨고 미리 보는 봄.

In the spring there are
many things to see.
A season for seeing
the as yet unseen.
The heart's eyes open,
see the future spring.

온몸으로 살아낸 하루는
삶의 이야기를 남긴다.
나만의 이야기가 없는 하루는
살아도 산 날이 아니다.

A day lived thoroughly
leaves behind tales of life.
A day without tales of myself
was lived yet not lived.

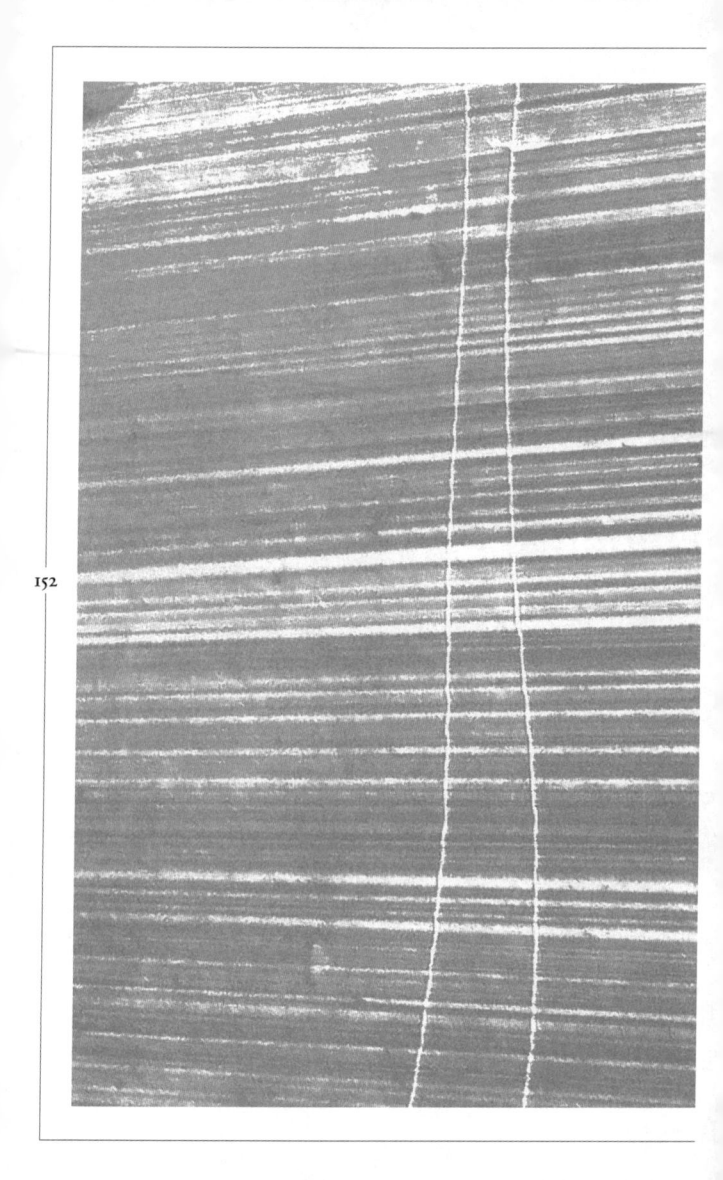

욕망은 절제될 수 없다.
더 높은 차원에서
전환될 수 있을 뿐이다.

Greed cannot be controlled.
It can only be shifted
from a higher level.

걷히지 않는 구름이 있겠어요.
잠들지 않는 폭풍이 있겠어요.
가시지 않는 불운이 있겠어요.

How could there be clouds
that do not clear?
How could there be storms
that do not fall asleep?
How could there be misfortunes
that do not cease?

무언가를 얻는 것보다 중요한 것은
나 자신을 잃지 않는 것이다.

More important than gaining something
is not losing myself.

좋은 디자인은
사물의 본질적 쓰임과
물질의 심장에 곧바로
이르게 하는 것.

Good design
is directly achieved
by the essential use of things,
the heart of material things.

절제된 우아함과
삼가한 자유로움.

Restrained elegance
and limited freedom.

혁명이란 새로운 것을
만드는 것만이 아니라
본성대로 돌려놓는 것이고
참모습을 되찾는 것이니.

What is called revolution
is not just a matter of
making new things.
It means returning them
to their original nature,
recovering
their original appearance.

오늘은 다르게.
나날이 새롭게.

Today, differently.
Every day, newly.

옳은 일을 하다가 한계에 부딪혀
여기서 그만 돌아서고 싶을 때,
고개 들어 살아갈 날들을 생각하라.
지금 스스로 그어버린 그 선이
평생 나의 한계선이 되리니.

When you come up against
a limit after doing what is right,
long to give up and turn back,
think of days when you will live
with head held high.
The line I draw for myself now
will become a boundary line
for the rest of my life.

두려운 것은 답을 틀리는 것이 아니라
내 안의 물음이 사라져버리는 것이다.

The things I dread is not
the answer being wrong,
it's the question inside me vanishing.

명궁은 표적보다
더 높은 곳을 향해 쏜다.

An expert archer
aims at a point above the target.

겸손한 자만이 당당할 수 있고
당당한 자만이 겸손할 수 있다.

Only someone humble
can be confident,
only someone confident
can be humble.

모든 진실은 현장에 있다.
현장이 변하면 진실도 변한다.

Every truth is in its place.
If the place changes,
the truth changes, too.

하나의 말은
그 말을 하는 순간
사건이 된다.

One word,
the moment it's spoken,
becomes an event.

이 짧은 한 장면을 만나기 위해
일생을 기다려온 그런 영화가 있다.

There are movies
I waited a whole lifetime for
in order to experience one short scene.

힘 들어야
힘이 들어온다.

Difficulty
brings strength.

182

비바람 속에서도
명랑한 얼굴로 피어나는
눈부신 꽃들에 경배!

A toast to the dazzling flowers
that blossom with cheerful faces
in the midst of wind and rain!

어린 날 새겨져 평생을 이끄는
좋은 습관을 물려주는 것이
최고의 유산이다.

Passing on good habits
acquired in childhood
that have guided a whole lifetime
is the best bequest.

그저 그런 책 백 권을 읽는 것보다
단 한 권의 책을 거듭 읽는 게 낫다.

Reading one book over and over
is better than reading
a hundred of that kind of books.

진정한 강함은 내적 강함이다.
모든 것이 무너져도
마음이 무너지지 않는 한
결코 무릎 꿇릴 수 없는 것이 인간이다.
마음만 서면 다시
일어설 수 있는 것이 인간이다.

True strength is inner strength.
To be human is never
to be brought to one's knees,
though everything collapses,
so long as the heart does not collapse.
To be human is being able to rise again
if only the heart remains standing.

긴 하루가 지나고 밤이 걸어올 때,
내가 돌아갈 자리가 있고
돌아갈 사람이 있다는 건
얼마나 큰 축복인가.

When night approaches
at the end of a long day,
what a blessing that there is
somewhere for me to go back to,
that there is
someone for me to go back to.

세상 누구와도 비교될 수 없는
나에게 하나뿐인 그 존재.
못나도 울 엄마, 못나도 울 아빠.

Those incomparable beings,
unique to me,
my homely mother,
my homely father.

사랑은 기꺼이 닳아가는 것.
조금은 지쳐있고 얼룩진 모습 그대로가
내 눈물겨운 사랑의 흔적이니.

Love is glad to start wearing out.
Simply looking slightly weary and stained
is the sign of my tearful love.

961

상처는 치유가 아닌
잉태의 과정이다.

A wound is a process of birth,
not of healing.

결코 변해서는 안 될 것을 지켜가기 위해
하루하루 치열히 변화해가야 한다.

In order to safeguard what must not change
we have to change intensely every day.

네가 자꾸 쓰러지는 것은
네가 꼭 이룰 게 있기 때문이야.
네가 다시 울며 가는 것은
네가 꽃피워낼 게 있기 때문이야.
힘들고 앞이 안 보일 때는
너의 하늘을 보아.

The reason
you keep falling down is
because there is something
you have to achieve.
The reason you
set off again weeping is
because there are flowers
you should bring to bloom.
When life is hard
and there is no way ahead,
look up at your sky.

정직한 절망이
희망의 시작이다.

Honest despair
is the beginning of hope.

자주, 그리고 환히 웃어요.
가끔, 그리고 깊이 울어요.

Often, brightly, I laugh.
Rarely, deeply, I weep.

놀이에 몰입한 아이는 재미마저 잊듯이
진정 행복한 사람은 행복을 묻지 않는다.

Just as a child absorbed in play
forgets about fun,
someone really happy
does not think about happiness.

아무리 많은 것을 경험해도
내면의 느낌으로 새겨지지 않는 것은
바람에 날리는 먼지처럼 흩어진다.

No matter how many things
we experience,
whatever is not inscribed
as an inner feeling is scattered
like dust in the wind.

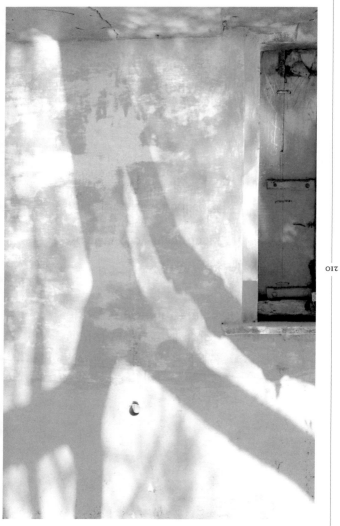

진가를 알아보는 것이 지혜다.
사물의 진가를 알아보는 안목眼目.
사람의 진가를 알아보는 식별識別.

Recognizing true worth is wisdom.
Discrimination to recognize
the true worth of things,
discernment to recognize
the true worth of people.

누구나 실수할 수 있다.
실수를 인정하지 않는 것이
최악의 실수다.

Anyone can make a mistake.
Not admitting one's mistake
is the worst kind of mistake.

정치인에게 권력을 빼보라.
부자에게서 돈을 빼보라.
유명인에게 인기를 빼보라.
빼버리고 남은 것이 바로 그다.

Take power from politicians,
take money from the wealthy,
take popularity from the famous,
and what's left after that is
precisely who they are.

사랑만큼의 실력을.
실력만큼의 사랑을.

Ability as great as love.
Love as great as ability.

다 함께 추웠던 겨울보다
봄날의 그늘이 더 서러워.

A spring day's shadows are sadder
than winter when all were cold together.

나는 만 사람의 찬사와 비난보다
그대 한 사람이 지켜보는 걸 두려워한다.
만 사람의 사랑을 구하기보다
그대 한 사람이 떠나가는 걸 두려워한다.

More than ten thousand people's praise
and blame, I fear the way you,
one individual, observe me.
Rather than gaining
the love of ten thousand, I fear you,
one individual, leaving me.

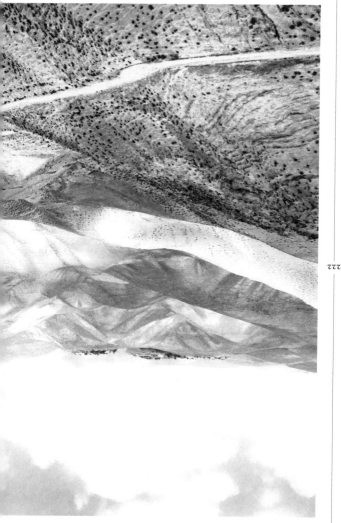

시련 속에서
계시가 온다.

In times of trial
revelation comes.

용기를 내라.
용기는 도끼날과 같아
쓰면 쓸수록 빛난다.

Be brave.
Courage is like an axeblade.
The more it's used,
the brighter it shines.

사람이 미워질 때면 울려오는 어머니 말씀.
'세상에 그런 사람도 하나 있어야제.'
'그인들 그러고 싶어서 그리했겠느냐.'

At times when someone becomes hateful,
Mother's words:
'There has to be one such person in the world.'
'They act like that though they don't want to.'

하늘이 흐르는 구름을 붙잡지 않듯이
그렇게 집착하지 말고 흘러갈 게 있다.

Just as the sky
does not cling to passing clouds,
there are things
that pass without clinging.

나는 얼마나 열심히 멀어져 왔던가.
열심히 공부해 진리에서 멀어지고
열심히 일해서 삶에서 멀어지고
너무 많이 나에게서 멀어져 왔다.

How busily I have moved away.
Studying hard, I moved away from the truth,
working hard, I moved away from life,
I have moved too far away from myself.

지구별에 놀러 온 아이야.
너는 맘껏 놀고 기뻐하고 사랑하라.
그리고 네 삶을 망치는 것들과 싸워가라.

You child come to play on this globe.
Play, rejoice, love to your heart's content,
and fight with everything that spoils your life.

우주는 집우宇, 집주宙.
나의 집은 우주다.

In Chinese characters,
宇宙 means 'universe,'
each character means 'house,'
so the universe is my home.

우리 인생에는
각자가 진짜로 원하는 무언가가 있다.
나에게는 분명, 나만의 다른 길이 있다.

In our lives,
there is something which
each of us really wants.
For me, certainly,
I have my own different path.

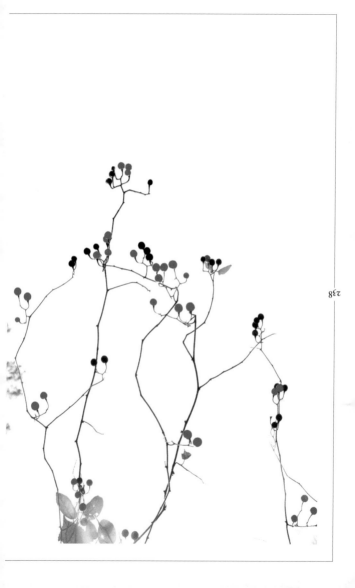

패션은 사상이다.

Fashion
is a way of thinking.

생활이 고달프다 하여
함부로 살아가지 않기를.
가난과 불운이 내 마음까지
흐리게 하지 않기를.

May you never live recklessly just
because life is tough.
May poverty and misfortune never
cloud your heart.

상처받고 있다는 건
내가 살아있다는 것.
상처받고 있다는 건
내가 사랑한다는 것.
그대, 상처가 희망이다.

The fact of being wounded
means that I'm alive.
The fact of being wounded
means that I am loving.
You, wound, are hope.

밤하늘에 가장 빛나는 별은
북극성도 명왕성도 아니다.
인공위성이다.
너무 번쩍이는 빛을 경계하라.

The brightest star
in the night sky
is neither Polaris nor Pluto.
It's an artificial satellite.
Beware of lights
that shine too bright.

중력을 거스른 인간의 직립,
저항은 존재의 숙명이다.

Defying gravity allows us
to stand upright,
resistance is each one's destiny.

젊음이라면
한번은 미쳐야 한다.
한번은 바쳐야 한다.

If it's youth
it must once go mad.
It must once sacrifice itself.

인생길을 비추는 두 개의 등불이 있다.
하나는 내가 가야 할 목적지에서 비추고
하나는 내가 시작한 첫마음에서 빛난다.

Two lamps shine out along our path.
One shines from the destination
I have to reach,
the other from the heart with which
I first set out.

주어진 길 밖의 모든 길이 그대의 것이다.
심어진 꿈 밖의 모든 꿈이 그대의 것이다.

All paths except given paths are yours.
All dreams except rooted dreams are yours.

아무리 위대한 현자도
사심이 깃들면
한순간에 바보가 된다.

No matter how wise someone is,
when self-interest comes sneaking
in a flash he's a fool.

남을 딛고 앞서가기보다
나를 이겨 도약하기를.

Rather than trampling on others
to get ahead,
controlling and leaping over myself.

어머니 안에는 바다가 있었네.
나를 품어 기른 바다가 있었네.
아버지 안에는 산맥이 있었네.
나를 올려 세운 산맥이 있었네.

Inside Mother there was an ocean,
an ocean that embraced and nourished me.
Inside Father there was a mountain range,
a mountain range that raised me aloft.

사랑을 받으면서도
그 사랑을 제 한 몸에 가두는 사람은
사랑의 배신자다.

People who receive love
then keep it locked up inside themselves
are traitors to love.

그가 경외하는 이들이 그를 말해준다.
그가 경멸하는 자들이 그를 말해준다.

Those who he worships indicate who he is.
Those who he disdains indicate who he is.

적은 것으로 할 수 있는 것을
많은 것으로 이루는 것처럼
바보같은 일은 없다.

There is nothing more foolish
than achieving with much
what can be done with little.

신독愼獨, 홀로 있어도 삼가함.
홀로 있을 때의 모습이
진짜 그의 모습이다.

Being steadfast,
unshaken though alone.
The way we are seen when alone
is the way we truly are.

잘못을 되돌릴 수는 없지만
잘못을 바로잡을 수는 있다.

A mistake cannot be undone
but a mistake can be put right.

오늘 하루
얼마나 감동했는가.
얼마나 감사했는가.
얼마나 감내했는가.
그리하여 얼마나
더 나아진 내가 되었는가.

Today
how much was I moved?
How thankful was I?
How much did I endure?
So how much
did I become a better I?

인생이 막막한 사막길 같을지라도
막막함이 사라지고 나면 숨막힘뿐인 것을.

Even if life is like a boundless desert path,
once vastness vanishes,
all that remains is suffocating.

우리 할머니 최고의 욕.
주변머리 없는 이. 멋없는 이. 얼간이.
일과 멋과 얼이 그 자신이라는 말씀.

Our grandmother's worst curses:
Scissorbill! Drab! Dummy!
Saying that everything,
work, style, spirit, are the same as oneself.

좋지 않은 걸 보면 눈을 씻고 가자.
나쁜 말을 들으면 귀를 씻고 가자.

On seeing something that is not good,
let's wash our eyes and go.
On hearing bad words,
let's wash our ears and go.

278

시간은 모든 것을 쓸어가는 비바람.
시간은 아름다움을 빚어내는 거장의 손길.
오래된 것들은 다 아름답다.

Time is a storm that sweeps everything away.
Time is the hand of a master creating beauty.
Old things are all beautiful.

돈으로는 살 수 없는 것을
얼마나 많이 가졌는가.

How much have I had
of what money cannot buy?

매일 아침 일어나서
내가 하는 일은 이것이다.
이부자리를 정돈하는 일.
오늘 죽을 각오로 살아가는
나의 유언장이기에.

There is something I do
every morning, on rising.
I make my bed.
As I live today resolved to die,
that is my last will and testament.

좋은 부모가 되려고 안달하기보다
먼저 좋은 사람이 되기.
좋은 삶을 살아 보이기.

Rather than worrying about
becoming a good parent,
first becoming a good person,
showing what it is to live a good life.

나무가 땅의 속박을 벗어나는 건
자유가 아닌 죽음이듯
진정한 자유란 '함께하는 혼자'로
숲 속에 선 푸른 나무다.

Just as a tree casting off
earth's shackles
is not freedom but death,
true freedom, 'being alone together,'
is a green tree standing in a forest.

기를 쓰지 말고
마음을 써라.

Do not strive too hard.
Strive with your heart.

사랑은 대가도 없고 보상도 없는 것.
사랑은 사랑 그 자체로 충분한 것.

Love has neither price nor reward.
Love is enough in itself.

어젯밤 비가 내리고
하늘엔 먼지 하나 없어라.
나도 어젯밤 많이 울었다.

Last night it rained a lot
and there is
not a speck of dust in the sky.
Last night I wept a lot.

만나는 사람마다
마음과 정성을 다하기를.
내 영혼이 얼지 않는
샘물처럼 솟아나기 위해.

Every time I meet someone,
I will make every effort
to ensure that my soul gushes
like a never-freezing spring.

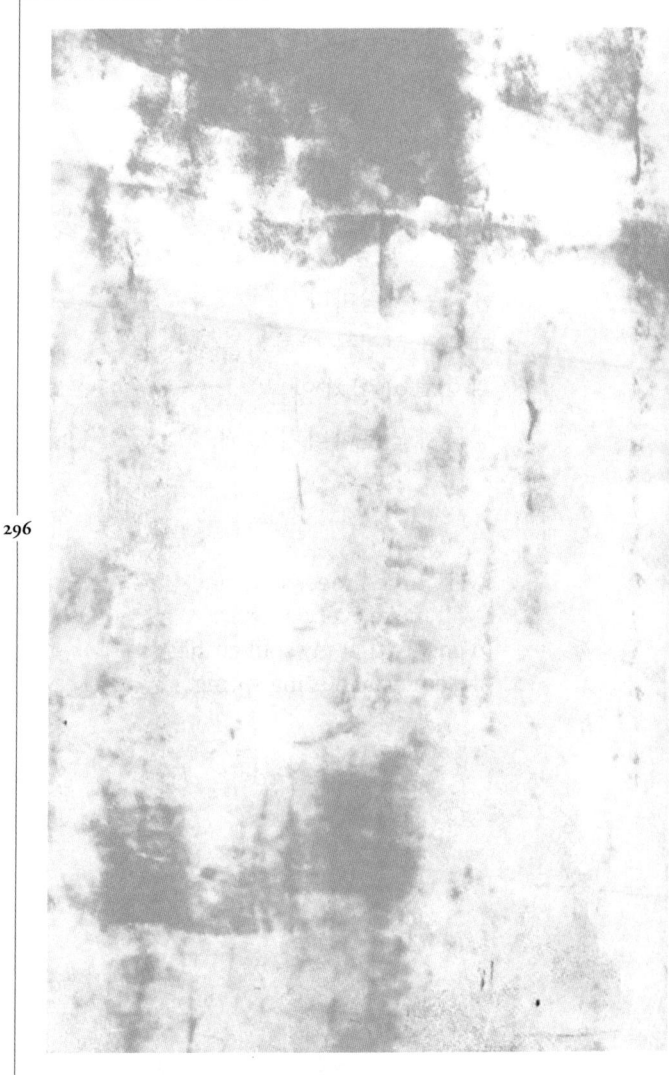

아름다운 것들에는 치열함이 어려 있다.
아름다움은 치열한 앓음에서 탄생한다.

Beautiful things have a trace of intensity.
Beauty is born of intense pain.

사람은 본디 누구나 착하다.
아직 나쁜 상황을 만나기 전까지는.

Originally, each person is good.
So long as they do not encounter
bad situations.

권력은 중독이다.
자본은 중독이다.
인기는 중독이다.
질투는 중독이다.
남탓은 중독이다.

Power is an addiction.
Capital is an addiction.
Popularity is an addiction.
Envy is an addiction.
Blaming others is an addiction.

대지에 두 발을 딛고 살아온 건강한 몸과
쉽게 좌절하지 않는 영혼을 가진 이에게는
푸른 기운이 흘러나온다.

For anyone who has a healthy body
that walks with two feet on the earth,
and a soul that is not easily discouraged,
a stream of green energy comes flowing.

하르르 하르르 꽃잎이 질 때면
지는 꽃잎 사이로 하늘을 보다
이대로 그만 죽어도 좋았다.

As petals flutter and fall
I see the sky between the falling petals.
I would like to die like that.

사랑은, 나의 시간을 내어주는 것이다.

Love is giving out my time to someone.

우리 모두는
자기 삶의 연구자가 되어야 한다.
내가 나 자신을 연구하지 않으면
누군가 나를 연구하고 써먹는다.

All of us
have to study our own lives.
For if I don't study myself
somebody will study me
then gobble me up.

나에게만 다르게 들리는 소리가 있다.
내 목소리다.
나는 나 자신에게 늘 착각이다.

There's a sound
that is different only to myself,
my own voice.
I am always an illusion to myself.

넘치는 지식보다
비움의 지혜를.

Rather than
overflowing knowledge,
the wisdom of emptiness.

나를 이토록 떨림으로 뒤흔드는 노래.
나를 단숨에 그 시절로 데려가는 노래.
한순간 나를 울게 하고 살게 하는 노래.
그런 단 한 곡의 노래가 있다.

A song that shakes me
and makes me tremble.
A song that transports me
back to those days in a flash.
A song that in a moment
makes me cry, makes me live.
There is just one such song.

일을 위한 삶인가
삶을 위한 일인가.

Living for work
or working to live?

'바빠서'라는 건 없다.
나에게 우선순위가 아닐 뿐.

There is no such thing
as 'being busy.'
It's just that
I have no order of priorities.

길을 잘못 들어섰다고
슬퍼하지 마라, 포기하지 마라,
삶에서 잘못 들어선 길이란 없으니.
모든 새로운 길이란
잘못 들어선 발길에서 찾아졌으니.

Don't be sad, don't give up
because you think
you've taken the wrong path.
In life there is no wrong path.
Every new path is found by taking steps
along the wrong path.

갈라진 두 마음으로는
하나도 제대로 이루지 못한다.

Two divided hearts
can never really become one.

우리가 아이들에게 빼앗아버린
가장 소중한 것은 '결여'의 힘이다.
결여만이 줄 수 있는 간절함, 견디는 힘,
궁리와 분투, 강인한 삶의 의지다.

The most precious thing
we deprive children of
is the power of deficiency.
The eagerness, the power to endure,
reflection and struggle,
that only deficiency can give,
are the basis for a tenacious life.

하루아침에 바람이 바뀌듯
때가 되면, 하루아침이다.

Just as the wind changes suddenly,
one morning, the time will come.

좋은 사회로 가는 길은 없다.
좋은 삶이 곧 길이다.

There is no path
leading to a good society.
A good life is the path.

조용한 숲은 불타버린 숲이다.
조용한 강은 썩어가는 강이다.
민주주의는 늘 시끄러운 것.
살아있다면, 일어나 외쳐라.

A silent forest is a burned-out forest.
A silent river is a rotting river.
Democracy is always noisy,
so if you are alive, stand up and shout.

평온한 저녁을 위하여.

For a peaceful evening.

사랑은 나직하게.
나눔은 소리 없이.

Loving, gently.
Sharing, silently.

인생에서 최대의 비극은
삶의 수단에 집착하느라
삶의 목적을 잃어버리는 것이다.

In a human life,
the greatest tragedy
is to be so obsessed
with the means of living
that the goal of life is lost to view.

첫인상을 남길 기회는 한 번뿐이고
첫사랑의 떨림도 한 번뿐이듯
첫마음을 새길 시기는 한 번뿐이다.
젊은 날의 첫마음이 한 생을 비춘다.

We have only one chance
to make a first impression.
We only once experience
the thrill of first love.
Our hearts only once
make a first decision.
That first heart of our youthful days
sheds light for a lifetime.

아는 만큼 보이는 것이 아니다.
사랑한 만큼 보이는 것이다.

You do not see as much as you know.
You see as much as you have loved.

더 이상 뺄 수 없을 때까지
하나하나 빼 보라.
그때 꼭 해야만 하는 일이
새벽별처럼 떠오르니.

Little by little reduce
until nothing more can be reduced.
At that point what has to be done
will shine out like the morning star.

인생의 결정적인 네 가지 인연.
부모. 친구. 스승. 연인.
그리고 그 모든 걸 결정짓는
진정한 나 자신.

Life's four decisive relationships.
Parents, friends, teachers, lovers.
And playing a decisive role in all those,
my true self.

악은 갈수록 새로와지고 다양해지고,
평범해지고 다수결 속에 강력해진다.
나는 '악의 신비'를 지켜보고 있다.

As it goes on, evil grows new, diverse,
commonplace, a powerful majority.
I am observing the 'mystery of evil.'

조급한 자는 실상 태만한 자이고
태만한 자는 늘 조급할 수밖에 없다.

Any one impatient
is really being lazy.
Lazy people are always bound to be
impatient.

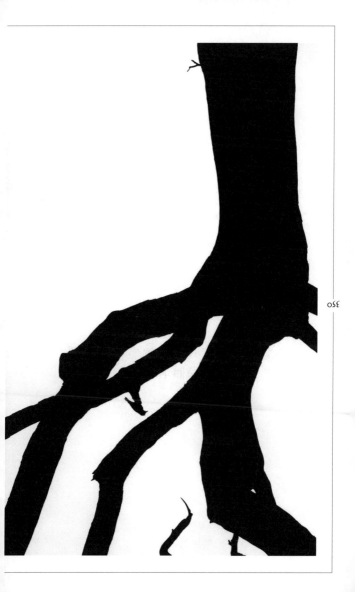

고생, 고苦는 생生이다.
고통 속에 무언가 탄생하고 있다.

A hard life is hard, and it is life,
when life is hard,
something is being born.

살아있는 한 희망은 끝나지 않았고
희망이 있는 한 삶은 끝나지 않는다.

So long as I am alive, hope does not end.
So long as there is hope, life does not end.

여름은 '열음'.
창문을 열고 옷깃을 열고
가슴마저 활짝 여는 계절.

Summer is a season of opening.
Opening windows, opening collars,
even opening wide the heart.

아무것도 아니었으나
모든 것이 두근대던 시절.
젊음은 좋은 것이다.

That age when everything,
even nothing special,
was thrilling.
Youth is good.

사랑한다고 말하지 않지만
사랑에 감싸여 있음을
느끼게 하는 이가 있다.

There are people
who do not say I love you
but who make you feel
that you are wrapped in love.

나 어떻게 살 것인가 막막할 때는
어떻게 살지 말 것인가를 생각하라.

When at a loss how I should live,
think about how not to live.

나에게 지옥이 있다면
여인과 아이가 없는 곳.
꽃과 나무와 시가 없는 곳.

Hell for me
is a place
with no women or children,
a place
with no flowers, trees, and poetry.

오늘은 한심閑心하게 지냈다.
아무것도 하지 않아 가득한 한심으로
긴 하루 생을 잘 살았다.

I spent a pathetic day today.
Fully pathetic, doing nothing,
I spent a long day well.

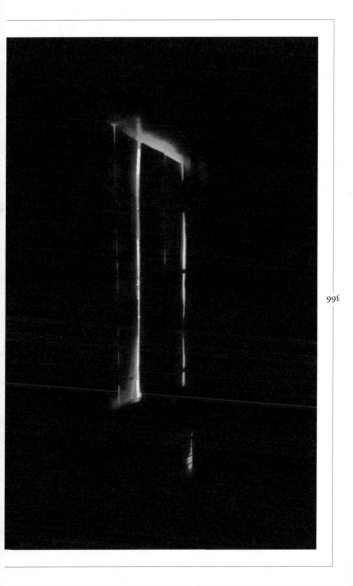

The perfection of evil
has the face of what is good.

악의 완성은
선이 얼굴을 갖는 것이다.

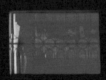

정말 좋은 영화는
영화가 끝나는 순간부터
나만의 영화가 시작된다.

A really good movie begins
as my own private movie
once the movie is over.

해결할 것이 있고
해소할 것이 있다.
풀지 않으면 쌓여가는 것과
놓아두면 풀려가는 것이 있다.

Some things can be solved,
some things can be resolved.
Some things pile up if not cleared away,
some things work out if left alone.

눈 앞의 등불을 끄지 않고는
하늘의 별빛을 볼 수 없다.
작은 것은 크고 깊은 것을
비출 듯 가리고 서 있으니.

Until the lamp before my eyes
was extinguished
I could not see the stars in the sky.
Small things, pretending to shine,
stand blocking great, deep things.

아이에게 좋은 것만 주는 부모는
불행히도 나쁜 부모다.

Parents who only give good things
to their children
are unfortunately bad parents.

혼 낸다는 것은
혼을 불러낸다는 것.
아 누가 나를 혼 내주나.

A spirited scolding
revives the spirits.
So who is making me
so disspirited?

오늘날의 대죄가 있다.
자유로운 탐욕.
정의로운 교만.
지혜로운 위선.

Such are today's deadly sins.
Free greed.
Just pride.
Wise hypocrisy.

'어찌할 수 없음'은 기꺼이 받아들이고
'어찌해야만 함'은 최선을 다해 분투하라.

Accept what cannot be helped,
fight with all your might against
what must be done.

삶의 최종 목적지에서 바라본다면
지금의 고통은 신비한 계획 속의
어느 지점을 통과하고 있는 것인지 모른다.

Seen from life's final destination,
this moment's pain may be a passage
through a point in a mysterious plan.

바람은 보이지 않는 대지의 숨결.
음악은 보이지 않는 영혼의 탄식.

The wind is the world's invisible breath.
Music is the soul's invisible sigh.

삶에서는, 시간이 많은 사람이 부자다.

In life, anyone who has plenty of time is rich.

쌉쌀한 커피 한 모금.
그윽한 여운 한 모금.
인생의 고독 한 모금.

A sip of bitter coffee.
A sip of quiet seclusion.
A sip of life's solitude.

더 고귀한 일상을 창출하지 못하면
혁명이 아니다.
더 고유한 인격을 세워내지 못하면
혁명이 아니다.

If we cannot create a more noble life,
it is not a revolution.
If a more distinct personality
does not emerge,
it is not a revolution.

단순하게.
단단하게.
단아하게.

Simply.
Firmly.
Gracefully.

저항할 것에 순종하고
순명할 것에 저항하는 것을
어리석음이라 한다.

Obeying what should be resisted
and resisting what should be obeyed
is considered folly.

돌 같은 믿음.
돌 같은 침묵.
돌 같은 정진.
돌에서 꽃이 핀다.

Stone-like trust.
Stone-like silence.
Stone-like abstinence.
Flowers bloom
from stones.

세상이 나를 몰라준다고 원망하기보다
내실보다 더 알려진 것을 두려워한다.

I fear being better known than I deserve
rather than being upset
because the world does not understand me.

위기와 혼란의 한가운데서
누가 조용히 생각하는 이를 가졌는가.

Amidst crisis and confusion
did anyone ever have
a quietly thinking person?

사람은 인생의 모든 시기에
잘 나가기 어려운 것처럼
인생 내내 헤매기도 어렵다.

Just as it hard
at every moment of life
for people to set off well,
so too it is hard for life to go astray.

길게 보면
지금 좋은 게 좋은 게 아니고
지금 나쁜 게 나쁜 게 아니다.

Seen at length,
good things now are not so good,
bad things now are not so bad.

하루아침에 떠오르는 것은 없다.
하루아침에 무너지는 것은 없다.
조금씩 조금씩 꾸준히 나빠지고
조금씩 조금씩 꾸준히 좋아질 뿐.

Nothing rises in a single night.
Nothing collapses in a single night.
Simply, little by little, steadily they go bad
and little by little, steadily they get better.

살다 보면 존재는 의식을 배반한다.
인간은 그가 사는 대로 되어간다.

As life goes on,
being betrays consciousness.
Each becomes that while living.

옷장엔 옷들이 가득한데
정작 입을 옷이 없다.
책장엔 책들이 가득한데
지금 읽을 책이 없다.
결정적인 단 하나가 없다.

The wardrobe is full of clothes
but in fact there's not one
for me to wear.
The bookshelf is full of books
but now there's not one
for me to read.
Not one that is decisive.

참된 독서란
자기 강화의 독서가 아닌
자기 소멸의 독서다.

True reading
is not reading
for self-enhancement
but reading
for self-extinction.

심장을 팔아 물질을 채우지 말고
물질의 심장을 꽃피우며 살기를.

May we live bringing flowers to bloom
in the heart of things,
not selling our hearts
to accumulate things.

방향이 잘못 잡혀 있다면
빠르게 달려갈수록
빠르게 이탈해간다.

If you set off
in the wrong direction,
the faster you go
the faster you go off course.

인간의 노동과 영혼과 생의 시간이 담긴
돈을 벌기란 얼마나 힘든 것인가.
그 돈을 그러모은 부유한 자의 영혼이
행복하기란 얼마나 힘든 것인가.

How hard money-earning is, filled with
the time of peoples' labors, souls, lives.
How hard it is for the soul of the wealthy
raking in that money to be happy.

산정에 올라야 산맥이 보이고
산에서 나와야 산이 보인다.

A mountain range
can only be seen from the summit,
but to see a mountain
you have to leave it.

타인을 속이는 순간, 나는 안다.
나 자신을 먼저 속였다는 것을.

When I deceive someone, I realize
that I first deceived myself.

호랑이가 곶감을 무서워하는 것은
곶감이 뭔지 모르기 때문이다.
아는 건 그리 두렵지 않다.
무지가 두려움을 부른다.

The reason the tiger fears
the dried persimmon
is because it does not know what it is.
What we know is not so frightening.
Ignorance invites fear.

목적지는 저 먼 어딘가가 아니다.
그곳에 이르는 한 걸음 한 걸음이 목적지다.

The destination is not somewhere far away.
You reach it step by step.

내 안에는 죽은 이들이 살고 있다.
내 가슴은 광활한 탄생의 묘지다.

Those who have died are alive within me.
My breast is a vast graveyard of birth.

사람은 사람을 알아봐야 한다.
누구와 선을 긋나.
누구와 손을 잡나.
이로부터 모든 게 달라진다.

One person must appreciate another.
Start to draw a line with someone.
Hold hands with someone.
Then everything changes.

430

시인은 맨 처음 말하거나
최후에 말하는 사람이다.

A poet is one
who speaks first
or last.

여행을 떠날 땐 혼자 떠나라.
그러나 돌아올 땐 둘이서 오라.
낯선 길에서 기다려온
또 다른 나를 만나
둘이서 손잡고 돌아오라.

When you set out on a journey,
set out alone.
But when you return,
come with another.
Having met another self
waiting on some unfamiliar street,
come holding hands,
the two of you together.

삶을 허겁지겁 살지 않기.
생의 정수만을 음미하며 살기.

Not rushing through life.
Living savoring the essence of life.

정말 좋은 옷차림은
거울 앞에서 이게 나지, 한번 웃고
방문을 나서면 시선조차 잊어버리는 것.
좋은 옷은 빛의 날개니까.

Being really well dressed
is a matter of looking in the mirror,
saying 'this is what I am'
smiling, leaving the room and forgetting the sight.
For good clothes are wings of light.

죽는 날까지 자기 안에
소년 소녀가 살아있기를.

May the young boy or girl
within each one
remain alive until you die.

타인의 인정에 안달하고
거기에 길들여져 갈수록
자신을 잃어버리고 만다.

The more we worry
about others' approval
and depend on it,
the more we lose ourselves.

등에 진 짐이 무거울수록
깊은 발자국이 새겨진다.

The heavier the burden
on my back
the deeper my footprints.

나로 가득 차 숨 쉴 수조차 없는 마음에
푸른 바람이 드나들도록.
비우지 않는 종은 울릴 수 없으니.

Let a fresh breeze circulate
in a heart so full of self it cannot breathe.
A bell that is not empty cannot ring.

정점에 달한 양陽은
음陰을 위해 물러난다.

When Yang
reaches its height
it makes way for Yin.

448

성장에서
성숙으로.

From growth
to maturity.

태양을 가리는 데는
지구를 덮을 만큼의 장막이 필요치 않다.
눈동자를 가릴 손바닥이면 충분하다.

To blot out the sun there is no need
for a curtain to cover the world.
The palm of a hand covering
the eye is enough.

나는 사랑의 상처를 지닌 자를 사랑했다.
그러나 상처로 자신을 잃어버린 사람은
동정할 순 있어도 사랑할 순 없었다.

I loved one bearing love's wounds.
But when it was someone
who had lost himself in the wounds
I could not love them,
though I could sympathize.

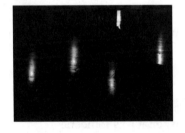

454

예술가의 타락은 이로부터 시작된다.
이익을 밝히는 것.
권력과 손잡는 것.
대중을 따르는 것.

This is how an artist falls:
Pointing the way to profit,
holding hands with power,
following the public mood.

열리면서도 닫힌.
닫히면서도 열린.

Closed but opening.
Open but closing.

나에게 실패보다 더 무서운 것은
의미 없는 성공이다.

What I fear more than failure
is meaningless success.

460

언젠가 어느 날인가
하늘이 나를 거두어가시는 날
지상에서 흘린 눈물만큼
웃음지며 떠나갈 수 있기를.

No matter when that day comes,
on the day when Heaven harvests me,
I hope I shall depart smiling as much
as I shed tears on earth.

말은 침묵을 낳지 못하지만
깊은 침묵이 없이는
살아있는 말이 나올 수 없다.

Words cannot give birth to silence
but without deep silence
living words cannot emerge.

저에게 최소한의 것만을 허락하소서.
최소한의 물질에서 최대한의 기쁨을.
최소한의 지식에서 최대한의 지혜를.
최소한의 관계에서 최대한의 사랑을.

Grant me
just a minimum of everything.
Maximum joy
with a minimum of things.
Maximum wisdom
with a minimum of knowledge.
Maximum love
with a minimum of relationships.

몸이 고달픈 건 견딜 수 있었다.
마음이 괴로운 건 견딜 수 없었다.

The body could endure
what was tiring.
The heart could not endure
what was distressing.

인간의 하루는 밤에 결산된다.
인간의 영혼은 밤에 시작된다.
밤의 시간을 낭비하지 마라.

Each person's day
is evaluated by night.
Each person's soul
begins by night.
Don't waste your night.

조로한 젊음을 보는 것만큼 슬픈 일은 없다.
미숙한 어른을 보는 것만큼 슬픈 일은 없다.

Nothing is sadder than
seeing prematurely aged youth.
Nothing is sadder than
seeing an immature adult.

인간은 힘을 가진 존재다.
살아있다면 뭐라도 해야 하고
가진 힘을 써야만 하는 존재다.
쓰이지 못한 힘은 억제된 만큼
반드시 어딘가로 무섭게 분출된다.

Humans are beings with strength.
While they live, they are beings
who have to do something,
have to use their strength.
If the strength they cannot use
is repressed it will burst out
fearfully somewhere.

내 인생에 가장 소중한 그 일을
지금 바로 시작한다면.

If I were to begin right now
my life's most precious task.

살아있는 모든 것은
익어가는 시간이 필요하다.
제 속도로. 깊이깊이.

All living things
need time to ripen
at their own pace. In depth.

수많은 고통 중에 가장 큰 고통은
나 홀로 버려져 있다는 느낌.
인간은 세계 전체가 등을 돌려도
속마음을 나누고 나를 믿어주는
단 한 사람이 곁에 있다면,
그 사랑이면 살아지는 것이다.

Among the many kinds of pain,
the greatest pain is feeling
that I am abandoned.
Even if the whole world turns its back,
so long as there's one person
there beside me
sharing innermost feelings and trusting me,
so long as that love is there, I'm alive.

고난은 우리 영혼의 맥박이다.

Pain is our soul's pulse.

과거를 팔아 오늘을 살지 말 것.
미래를 위해 오늘을 살지 말 것.

Don't sell the past to live today.
Don't live today for the sake of tomorrow.

도달할 수 있는 꿈은
이미 꿈이 아니다.

A dream
that can be achieved
is no dream at all.

권력은 사람을 두 번 바꾼다.
권력을 잡기 위해 스스로 변하고
권력을 잡고 나면 그 힘에 변한다.
한 번은 기대 속에.
한 번은 배신 속에.

Power changes people twice.
Intent on seizing power,
they change,
then after seizing power,
they change into that power.
Once in expectation.
Once in betrayal.

거대한 착각−
나만은 다르다.
이번은 다르다.
우리는 다르다.

Immense Illusions:
I alone am different.
This time is different.
We are different.

부딪쳐야 불꽃이 인다.
갈등에서 창조가 인다.

A match must be struck
to kindle a fire.
Creation kindles in conflict.

작은 도토리 한 알에
거대한 참나무가 들어있듯
내 안에는 더 큰 내가 숨 쉬고 있다.

Just as there is a vast oak tree
inside a tiny acorn,
inside myself a greater I is breathing.

멋은 무엇, 그 머시기,
그 무엇이 깃든 신비다.
멋있는 사람은 보이지 않는
그 무언가에 감싸여 있다.

Style, whatever it is,
is something
wrapped in mystery.
A stylish person is wrapped
in something invisible.

절정의 시간은 짧다.
바닥의 시간도 짧다.
삶은 최고와 최악의 순간들을 지나
유장한 능선을 오르내리며 가는 것.

Time at the top is brief.
Time at the bottom is brief.
Beyond the best and worst times
life climbs up and down lengthy slopes.

가을은 익어가는 계절.
쭉정이와 알갱이를 가려내는
엄정한 생의 계절.

Autumn is a season of ripening.
A severe season of life
distinguishing empty and full heads of grain.

길을 잃으면 길이 찾아온다.
길을 걸으면 길이 시작된다.
길은 걷는 자의 것이니.

If you lose your way,
the path comes seeking you.
If you start to walk, the path begins.
The path belongs to the walker.

밖으로 터지는 감탄의 힘이 있고
안으로 울리는 감동의 힘이 있다.

There is a power of admiration
that bursts outward
and there is a power of emotion
that resounds inwardly.

배우俳優는 사람人에 아닐非,
배우는 사람이 아닌 환영의 존재.
위대한 배우는
완전히 나를 잊고 그가 되게 하는
신이 깃드는 영매가 아닌가.
살아서 그런 배우를 만나는 건
인생의 보기 드문 축복이다.

In Chinese characters,
a filmstar is not a person,
a filmstar is a phantom, not a person.
A great filmstar
seems to be a medium possessed by a spirit
who makes me forget myself
and become the star.
Meeting such a star in one's life
is a blessing rarely seen in a lifetime.

사람들이 나를 좋아해 주면 좋겠으나
무시하고 싫어해도 신경 안 써 난.
어쩌라고, 날 알지도 못하는 자들을.
세상의 칭찬과 비난에
좌우될 수 없다니까 난.

If people like me, that's nice,
but I don't worry
if they despise and dislike me.
So what? Why bother about people
who don't know me?
I cannot be influenced
by the world's praise or blame.

지는 하루를 슬퍼하지 말 일이다.
저 태양은 지는 것이 아니라
나를 향해 돌아오는 중이다.

There is no need to feel sad
at the end of the day.
That sun is not setting,
it's on its way back to me.

이 지상에 무엇 하나
홀로 이룬 것은 없다.
이 세상에 누구 하나
홀로 빛나는 건 없다.

No matter
what I do on earth,
nothing is achieved alone.
Nobody in this world
shines alone.

고맙다 애썼다 장하다.
최선을 다해 익어온
그 마음을 안다.

Thanks.
You worked hard.
Admirable.
I know a heart
which had matured,
doing its very best.

비바람 치는 길을 걸어보지 못한 사람은
길의 절반도 걸어보지 못한 사람이다.

Anyone unable to walk
along a windswept path
is someone unable to walk halfway.

신은 건강의 비결을
발바닥과 대지에 반쪽씩 써넣었으니.
그들이 입맞춤할 때 강녕하리라.

God writes the secret of health
midway between the soles and the ground.
As they kiss, we grow healthy and peaceful.

좋은 동행자가 함께하면
그 어떤 길도 멀지 않은 법이다.

So long as we have
a good companion,
no journey lasts too long.

씨앗을 쥔 손은 힘차다.
미래를 쥔 손은 힘차다.
그대, 씨앗만은 팔지 마라.

A hand holding seeds
is powerful.
A hand holding the future
is powerful.
Don't only sell seeds.

문제아는
문제의식이 많은 아이.
세상을 달리 보는 아이.
문제아가 문제의 세상을 바꾼다.
힘내라 문제아!

A problem child
is a child with a critical mind,
a child who sees the world differently.
A problem child changes
the problematic world.
Bear up, problem child!

한 생에 드높은 서원誓願 하나
가슴에 품고 살아야 하지 않겠나.

Surely we should live
cherishing in our hearts
a lofty vow for our whole lifetime?

소유보다 중요한 건 쓰임이듯
얼굴보다 중요한 건 표정이다.
외모는 타고나는 것이지만
표정과 자태는 스스로 지어가는
인간 그 자신의 작품이다.

Using is more important than owning.
The expression is
more important than the face.
Our outward appearance
we are born with
but the expression and looks
are the work of each individual person.

몸은 점점 늙어가는데
마음은 영영 젊다는 건
저주인가 축복인가.

The body slowly ages
while the heart
remains perpetually young.
Is that a curse or a blessing?

갈아놓은 칼은
쓰게 마련이다.

It's natural to use
a sharpened sword.

비록 전쟁의 세상에 살지만
내 안에 전쟁이 살지 않기를.

Though living
in a world of warfare,
may I never know
warfare within myself.

자장자장 우리 아가.
잘 자거라 우리 아가.
지상에서 가장 욕심 없는 노래.
오늘도 지구의 골목길에 흐르는
눈물도 자장자장.
공포도 자장자장.
배고픔도 자장자장.

Rockaby baby, little child.
Sleep well, little child.
The most unselfish song in the world,
echoing again today
down Earth's alleyways:
Rockaby tears,
rockaby fears,
rockaby hunger, too.

나만 천국으로 가라 하면
나는 차라리 지옥으로 갈 것입니다.

If you tell only me to go to Heaven,
I shall surely go to Hell.

사랑은 했는데
이별은 못했네.
사랑할 줄은 알았는데
이별할 줄은 몰랐네.
사랑도 다 못했는데
이별은 차마 못하겠네.

I loved
but could not part.
I knew how to love,
but knew not how to part.
I could not love fully
so I shall
never be able to part.

좋은 마음으로 좋은 일들을
오래오래 해나가면 그렇게 되어간다.
'좋은 사람에게 좋은 일이'.

If you do good things with a good heart
for a very long time, you will become so.
'Good things for good people.'

우리가 세워야 할 것은 계획이 아니다.
확고한 삶의 원칙이다.
나머지는 다 믿고 맡겨두기로 하자.
계획의 틈새와 비움의 여백 사이로
여정의 놀라움과 인연의 신비가 찾아오리니.

What we have to make are not plans.
It's a firm rule of life.
Let trust and entrust all the rest.
For between the cracks in plans
and the blanks in voids,
come the wonder of journeying
and the mystery of relationship.

홀로일 때 충만하지 못하면
함께여도 충분하지 못하다.

If you cannot be satisfied when alone,
you cannot be satisfied even together.

사람을 버리는 두 가지 길이 있다.
책을 읽지 않는 것.
책을 많이 읽는 것.

Two ways of losing your personality.
Not reading any books.
Reading many books.

머리로 외우고 익힌 지식은 쉬이 잊혀진다.
몸으로 부딪쳐 깨친 이치는 오래 새겨진다.

Knowledge memorized with the head
is easily forgotten.
Common sense collided with and perceived
with the body remains long inscribed.

잘나고 이쁜 거야 누구라도 좋아하지만
결여를 있는 그대로 받아들이고 사랑하는 건
위대한 사람만이 할 수 있다.

Everyone likes what is fine and lovely
but accepting and loving what has deficiencies
is only possible for someone great.

가을볕이 너무 좋아
가만히 나를 말린다.
내 슬픔을, 상처난 욕망을,
투명하게 드러나는 살아온 날들을.

Autumn sunshine is so good.
Quietly it dries me out.
My sorrows, my wounded desires,
my only too clearly visible days of life.

일상을 이벤트로 만들지 말라.
담담한 일상 가운데
생의 비의秘意가 깃든다.

Don't make up an everyday life
composed of events.
Life's mystery dwells
in a serene everyday life.

식사보다 더 신비로운
일상의 의식이 있을까.
먹는 것과 먹는 이의 생명의 일치.
사랑과 신뢰로 이루어지는 삶의 잔치.
식사食事는 성사聖事다.

Is any of life's rituals
more mysterious than a meal?
Life's union of eaten and eater.
Life's party producing love and trust.
A meal is something sacred.

그 모든 것은 인연 따라 이루어진다.

Everything depends on relationships.

꽃과 열매를 보려거든 먼저 허리 숙여
땅심과 뿌리를 보살펴야 한다.

If you want to see flowers and fruit,
first you must bend
and nurture the earth and the roots.

전쟁은 총을 든 비즈니스이고
비즈니스는 총만 안 든 전쟁이다.

War is business with guns.
Business is war without guns.

사람들은 정당한 이유로
그릇된 일을 저지른다.

People act wrongly
for valid reasons.

몸은 모음이다.
온 우주가 모아진
내 한 몸이다.

The Korean word
for body means a gathering.
The whole universe
gathers into my one body.

지상의 모든 것은
한 톨의 씨앗에서 비롯되었다.

Everything on earth
began as a single seed.

아이들은 놀라워라.
가장 먼저 울고
가장 먼저 웃는
아이들은 놀라워라.

Children are amazing.
They are the first to cry
and the first to laugh.
Children are amazing.

틀려야 맞춘다.
깨져야 깨친다.

If it's wrong
it fits.
If it breaks
it's understood.

574

억압받지 않으면 진리가 아니다.
상처받지 않으면 사랑이 아니다.
저항하지 않으면 젊음이 아니다.

If it's not suppressed, it's not truth.
If it's not wounded, it's not love.
If it does not resist, it's not youth.

나의 행복은 비교를 모르는 것.
나의 불행은 남과 비교하는 것.
나에게는 오직 하나의 비교만이 있을 뿐.
어제의 나보다 더 나아진 나인가.

My happiness
is to know no comparisons.
My unhappiness
is comparing myself with others.
I have only one comparison.
Am I a better person today than yesterday?

열심이 지나치면
욕심이 된다.

Zeal taken to excess
turns into greed.

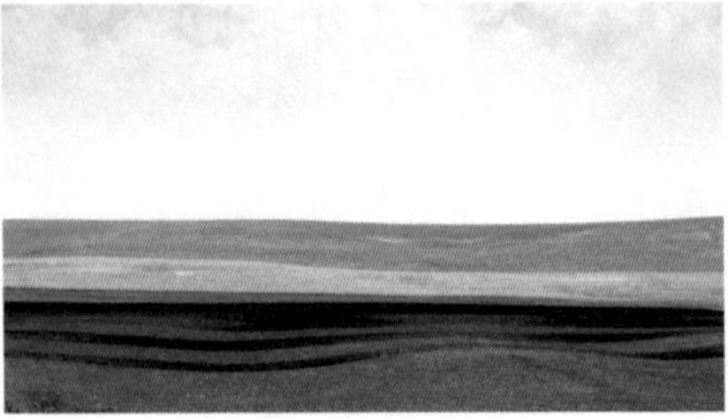

영양실조는
영양결핍만이 아니라
영양과잉이기도 하다.
지금, 결핍보다 무서운 건 과잉이다.

Malnutrition
is not only a lack of nutrition.
It is also excess nutrition.
Nowadays,
excess is more terrible than lack.

나눔만이 나뉨을 막을 수 있다.

Sharing alone can prevent division.

개인의 권리도 중요하나
인간의 도리가 먼저다.

Individual rights are important
but human duties come first.

누가 보아주지 않아도 나는 나의 일을 한다.
누가 알아주지 않아도 나는 나의 길을 간다.

Even with nobody looking,
I do my work.
Even with nobody acknowledging me,
I pursue my path.

우리 인생에 가장 위대한 계획자는 하늘이니.
부끄러운 것은 그 믿음을 잃어버리는 것이니.

The finest planner in our lives is Heaven.
Losing that belief is a source of shame.

고독은 견디는 것이 아니라
추구하는 것이다.

Solitude is something sought,
not endured.

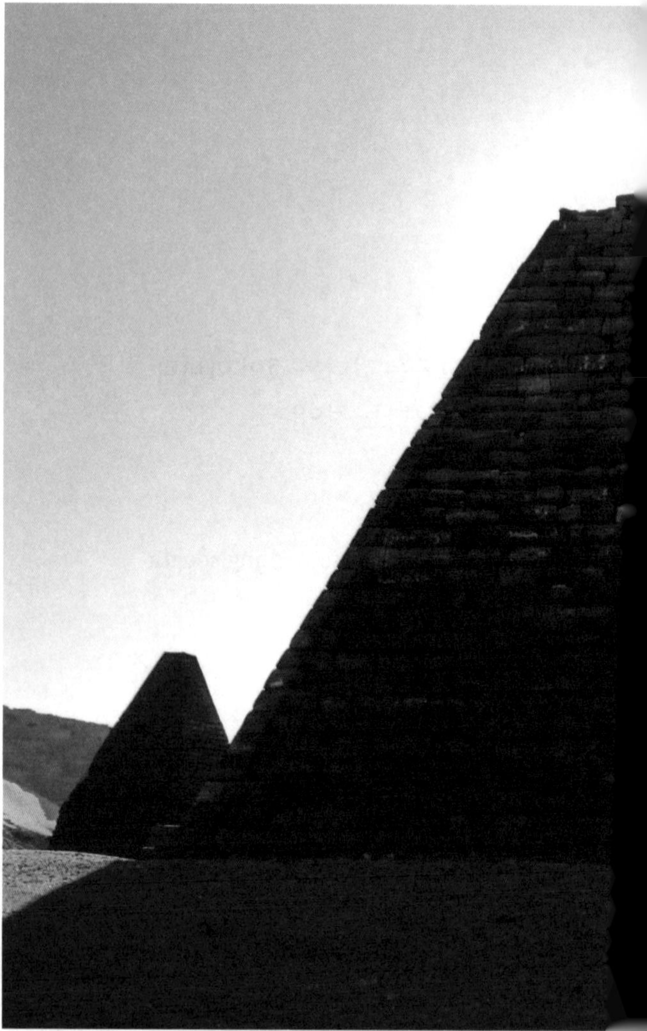

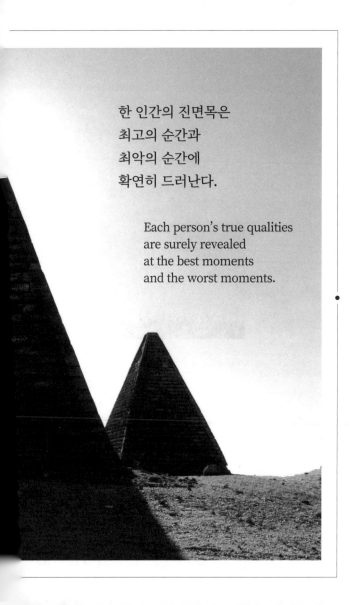

한 인간의 진면목은
최고의 순간과
최악의 순간에
확연히 드러난다.

Each person's true qualities
are surely revealed
at the best moments
and the worst moments.

말의 뿌리에 흙이 묻어 있지 않은 말.
말의 잎새에 눈물이 맺혀 있지 않은 말.
말의 꽃잎에 피가 배어 있지 않은 말을
나는 신뢰할 수 없으니.

Words without earth on their roots,
words without tears on their leaves,
words without blood on their petals,
those are words I cannot trust.

이 몸 안에 무엇이 익어가느라
이리 아픈가.
이 몸 안에 무엇이 태어나느라
이리 몸부림인가.

Is this pain
because something is ripening within me?
Is this struggling
because something is being born within me?

해 아래 존재한다는 한 가지 사실만으로도
키 큰 것들은 작은 것들에 그늘을 드리운다.
미안하다, 한 잎 두 잎 잎새를 떨구는 가을날.

One fact of life beneath the sun,
tall things overshadow little things.
An autumn day when leaves appologize,
dropping one by one.

갈수록 시간이 희망인 사람이 있다.
갈수록 시간이 쇠망인 사람이 있다.

For some people, time is hope.
For some people, time is ruin.

내 마음 깊은 곳에는
작은 방이 하나 있는데
눈물로 들어가 빛으로 나오는
심연의 방이 하나 있는데.

Deep within my heart
I have a little room,
a room that's an abyss
entered in tears,
emerging as light.

사랑의 상처를 치유하는 길은
더 사랑하는 일밖에 없다.

The only way to heal love's wounds
is to love yet more.

술은 가슴을 부딪히며 마시는 것.
차가운 술이 목을 타고 흘러내려
이 아픈 가슴이 뜨거워질 때,
가슴에서 가슴으로 건배!

Liquor is drunk heart to heart.
As cold liquor goes down the throat,
this aching heart grows warm
from heart to heart: Cheers!

같은 고난을 겪었다고
같은 잉태를 하는 게 아니다.

Saying we experienced
the same suffering
does not mean
that we experienced
the same pregnancy.

610

혁명가는 영원히 젊은 자.
진정한 혁명가는 혁명을 혁명한다.

A revolutionary is eternally young.
A true revolutionary revolutionizes revolution.

속셈 없는 마음으로.

A heart
without ulterior motives.

내가 없어도 꽃은 피고
아이들은 자라나고
세상은 돌아간다.
내가 없어도 내가 없어도.

Even without me,
flowers bloom,
children grow,
the world turns.
Even without me,
even without me.

세상의 끝에 오지가 있다.
아니다.
오지의 끝에 세상이 있다.

At the end of the world
there's a wilderness.
Not so.
At the end of the wilderness
there's the world.

618

바람아 불어라. 세차게 불어라.
내 뿌리는 더 깊어지고
내 씨앗은 더 멀리 날아갈 테니.

Blow, wind. Blow hard.
My roots will grow deeper,
my seeds will fly farther.

흐름을 따라가기보다
흐름이 되어가는 사람.

Rather than following the flow,
one who becomes the flow.

좋은 건축은 먼저
비움을 세우는 것이다.

A fine building
begins with emptiness.

아이가 부모의 젊음을 빨아먹고 자라듯
성장은 무언가를 잡아먹고 자란다.
멈출 때를 모르면, 성장이 죽음이다.

Just as a baby grows by sucking up
its parents' youth,
what does growth suck up to grow?
Unless it knows when to stop,
growth is death.

어떤 일을 하더라도 그 중심에는
사람이 있으면 좋겠습니다.

No matter what you do,
may people be at the center.

마음이 돌처럼 무거운 날.
고뇌가 바위처럼 누르는 날.
가을 강에서 물소리 듣는다.
강에서 돌들을 치워버리면
그 강은 노래를 잃어버리니.
돌 하나 품고 흐르는 저 강물처럼.

Days when the heart
is heavy as a stone.
Days when anguish
presses down like a rock.
Hear the sound of water rising
from the stream in autumn.
Remove the stones from the stream
and the stream will lose its song.
Like that stream
that flows embracing a stone.

쉼표가 없는 악보는 노래가 될 수 없다.
내 삶에 푸른 쉼표를.

A musical score with no rests
can never be sung.
My life's green rests.

세상이 병들기 전에
말이 먼저 타락한다.

Before the world falls sick,
words fall first.

어린 날 글자도 모르는 우리 할머니가 그랬지.
아가, 없는 사람 험담하는 곳엔 끼지도 말그라.
그를 안다고 떠드는 것만큼 큰 오해가 없단다.
그이한테 숨어있는 좋은 구석을 알아보고
토닥여 주기에도 한 생이 너무 짧으니께.
아가, 남 흉보는 말들엔 조용히 자리를 뜨거라.

When I was a child, our illiterate grandmother said:
Child, stay away from people
who gossip about those absent.
There's no greater misunderstanding than
chattering about people you claim to know.
Find out that person's hidden good points
since one lifetime is too short to strike out at people.
Child, when people speak ill of other, quietly leave.

더 깊이 성찰할수록
더 멀리 내다볼 것이다.

The deeper we look inward,
the farther ahead we can see.

진실로 내가 귀 기울이는 소리는
미약하고 희미한 소리들.
죽은 자의 말과 미래의 기척이다.

The sounds I really listen to
are weak, faint sounds,
words of the dead
and signs of the future.

우리 모두는
내가 사는 존재가 아니라
살려지고 있는 존재이다.

All of us
are not living beings
but beings coming alive.

사랑은 발바닥이다.
머리는 너무 빨리 돌아가고
마음은 날씨보다 변덕스럽지만
내 두 발이 그리로 갈 때
머리도 마음도
따라가지 않을 수 없으니.

Love is the soles of the feet.
The head turns too fast,
the heart is more capricious
than the weather
but when my feet go walking along
head and heart are bound to follow.

내 발끝의 '지경地境'이
내 정신의 '경지境地'다.

My toes' border
is my mind's stage.

나쁜 자가 정당해지는 유일한 길은
더 나쁜 자가 나타나는 것이다.

The only way
for a bad person to grow just
is for someone even worse to appear.

생의 고통은 위로로 사라지지 않는다.
우산을 쓴다고 젖은 날을 피할 수 없듯.

Life's pain does not vanish by consolation.
Just as using an umbrella
does not keep off heavy rain.

두려움에 사로잡히면
있는 힘도 못 쓰는 법.
담대하라, 담대하라.

When overwhelmed with fear
we cannot use the strength we have.
Be bold, be bold.

사람은 진실을 말하는 것보다
거짓을 말하는 것이 훨씬 힘들다.

Telling lies is much harder for people
than telling the truth.

선이 있고 악이 있는 것이 아니다.
선이 타락하면 악이 되는 것이다.

It is not that good exists and evil exists.
When what is good falls it turns into evil.

삶에는 준비가 없다.
삶에는 유보가 없다.
삶은, 지금 여기 이 순간이다.

There is no preparation for life.
There is no delay in life.
Life, is here now, this moment.

너무 재밌어진 세상에서
우리 조금 더 심심해지자.
심심해야 그리움이 살아나고
친구와 이웃을 찾게 되고
내 안의 창조성이 깨어날 테니.

In this so amusing world
let's grow a bit more bored.
Only with boredom
does yearning come alive,
making us look for friends
and neighbors,
so that the creativity
within me awakes.

선생先生님이란 앞서 사는 님.
먼저 진리를 살아내고
앞선 길을 걸어가는
선생님이 그리워라.

Our word for Teacher means
one who has lived ahead.
How I long for a teacher
who has first experienced truth,
gone walking along the path
ahead of me.

말은 삶으로 완성된다.

Words are made perfect
by life.

세상을 바꿀 수는 없을지라도
세상이 나를 바꾸지 못하도록
어둠 속에서 촛불을 켜라.

Even if I cannot change the world
light candles in the dark
so that the world cannot change me.

내 생의 기도는 단 하나,
땅에서와같이 하늘에서도.
삶에서와같이 영혼에서도.
나에서와같이 세상에서도.

There is only one prayer in my life:
As on earth, so too in heaven.
As in life, so too in the soul.
As in me, so too in the world.

668

삶은 기적이다.
인간은 신비이다.
희망은 불멸이다.

Life is a miracle.
Each human person is a mystery.
Hope is imperishable.

모든 시작의 시작은
원칙을 세우는 일이다.
그 시작을 보면 끝이 보인다.

The beginning of everything
is establishing principles.
If you see that beginning,
the end can be seen.

행복해야 한다고 집착하는 순간
곧바로 나머지 모든 생의 시간이
불행으로 전락하고 만다.

The moment I become convinced
that I have to be happy,
immediately all the rest of my life
falls into unhappiness.

좋은 농부에게 나쁜 땅은 없다.
좋은 사람에게 나쁜 환경은 없다.

To a good farmer no ground is bad.
To a good person no environment is bad.

가득한 소음과 소란 속에서
나는 혼자다, 혼자여야 한다.
사람들 속에 있어도 나는 혼자다.

Amidst abounding noise and uproar
I am alone, am bound to be alone.
Even amidst people, I am alone.

세상의 모든 우울이란
찬란한 비상의 기억을 품은
날개의 무거움.
날자, 우울이여.

All the world's gloom
is the weight of wings
embracing memories
of brilliant flight.
So, gloom, let's go flying on.

지구는 전속력으로 돌고 있지만
인간은 느끼지 못한다.
너무 거대하고 확실한 것은
알아채지 못한다.

The Earth is turning at high speed
but we cannot feel it.
Anything extremely large and confident
is imperceptible.

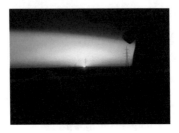

여행은 편견과의 대결이다.

A journey
is a struggle against prejudice.

바람이 부는 날이면
내 영혼은 달려 나간다.
어디로든, 어디로든,
그리운 네가 있는 쪽으로.

On a windy day,
my soul goes running.
Anywhere, anywhere,
toward you whom I yearn for.

아름다움을 추구하라.
그리고 그 빛에 둘러싸이라.

Demand beauty
and surround yourself
with that light.

권력이 없기 때문에
삶이 비참한 것이 아니다.
그 삶과 영혼이 빈곤하여
권력이 없이는
비참한 존재가 되는 것이다.

Life is not wretched
because it's powerless.
That life and soul,
being destitute,
become wretched,
being powerless.

자신을 믿지 못하는 사람을
누군들 믿을 수 있겠는가.

How can anyone trust
someone who cannot trust himself?

지켜야 할 것엔 늘 가시가 있지.
고귀한 것들엔 늘 가시가 있지.
강인한 사랑은 늘 가시가 있지.

What must be protected
always has thorns.
Noble things always have thorns.
Tenacious love always has thorns.

사막의 어린 나무는 한번 비가 내릴 때
그 짧은 몇 날 동안 훌쩍 자라버린다.
인생에도 그런 때가 있다.
나를 훌쩍 성숙시키는 도약의 때가.

If ever rain falls, a baby tree in a desert
grows rapidly for a few brief day.
There are days like that in human life, too,
days when we leap into maturity.

혼자서는 갈 수 없다.
웃으며 가는 길이라도.
함께라면 갈 수 있다.
눈물로 가는 길이라도.

We cannot keep on alone,
even along a path
that we can take with a smile.
We can keep on if we are together,
even along a path we take in tears.

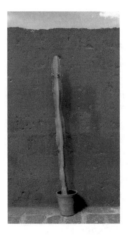

많다는 건 흔하다는 것.
많은 것은 없는 것이다.

Having much is common.
Having much is having nothing.

나는 나를 지나쳐 왔다.
나는 삶을 지나쳐 왔다.

I have passed myself by.
I have passed life by.

702

우리 모두는 별에서 온 아이들.
네 안에는 별이 빛나고 있어.

We are all children come from the stars.
A star is shining within you.

다른 요소가 다 좋다 한들,
영화는 영화만의 감동을 주어야 한다.

There may be other good factors
but a movie has to give
the movie's unique emotion.

어쩜 어디서든
오롯이 그 자신인
그런 패션이 있다.
그런 사람이 있다.

Anyway, somewhere
there is just
that kind of fashion,
the unique self,
that kind of person.

후지면 지는 거다.
타도할 수 없다면
낙후시켜라.

Inferiority is defeat.
If you cannot defeat
an enemy
make him lag behind.

이 땅에 살기 위하여.
사람으로 살기 위하여.
사랑으로 살기 위하여.

In order to live in this land.
In order to live a human life.
In order to live a loving life.

아, 우리도 하늘이 되고 싶다.
짓누르는 먹구름 하늘이 아닌
서로가 서로에게 푸른 하늘이 되는
그런 세상이고 싶다.

Ah, we too want to become a Heaven.
Not a Heaven with black clouds
weighing down,
we want to be a world
where each becomes
a blue heaven for others.

오만함과 비굴함,
난폭함과 나약함은
늘 한짝이다.

Arrogance
and obsequiousness,
violence and weakness,
always go together.

어떤 경우에도, 어떤 처지에도,
인간의 위엄을 잃지 말 것.

In any case, in every circumstance,
you should never lose human dignity.

얼굴은 얼골.
얼이 새겨진 골짜기.
그의 얼굴을 보면
그가 걸어온 길이 보인다.

The Korean word for face
suggests a valley,
a valley shaped by the soul.
At the sight of a person's face,
the path they have come by is visible.

아 고왔던 여인이여.
고단한 뒷모습의 내 어머니여.
수줍던 그 여인이여.

Ah, that once so lovely sweetheart.
My mother, her back so weary,
that once so shy sweetheart.

내가 이룬 빛나는 것들은
시든 꽃잎처럼 떨어져도
사랑, 사랑은 남아.

Though all my dazzling achievements
fall like faded petals,
love, love remains.

아쉽고 서운한 날이면,
이것으로 충분하다.
이만하면 넉넉하다.

On days of regret and sorrow,
this is enough.
This much is plenty.

남김없이 피고 지고.

Blooming and falling,
nothing left.

우리는 지나치게 다른 무언가가 되려고 한다.
사람은 자기 자신이 되는 것으로 충분한데.

We are too eager to become something different.
Becoming oneself is enough for anyone.

그녀가 사랑한 바다는
그녀를 영원히 간직하고선
끝없이 노래하네.
바위에 부딪치는 파도처럼
내 가슴을 치며 노래하네.

The sea that woman loved,
cherishing her forever,
sings of her without end.
I sing, beating my breast
like waves breaking on rocks.

자신의 심장을 잃지 않고는
사랑하는 이의 심장을 얻을 수 없다.

Any who fail to lose their heart
can never gain a lover's heart.

내가 찾는 간절한 것들은
지금 내가 욕망하는
반대쪽에서 걸어온다.

The dearest things I'm looking for
come walking from
the opposite direction
to what I desire now.

겨울은 겨우 사는 것.
보이는 것의 성장을 멈추고
보이지 않는 뿌리를 키우는 때.
안으로 응축하고 깊어지는 때.

In winter life is hard. It's a time
when growth ceases in what is visible
while invisible roots grow strong,
a time for inner condensation
and deepening.

나는 너를 결코 이해할 수 없다.
단지 온몸을 기울여 느낄 수 있을 뿐.

I cannot understand you at all.
I can only bend close and feel.

지금 있는 그대로 나누지 못하면
앞으로도 나눌 것이 없게 되리라.
그 마음은 갈수록 고갈되고 마니까.

If we cannot share now what we have,
later we will have nothing left to share
for that heart will grow increasingly depleted.

돈이 없이는 살 수 없고
돈이 있어도 삶이 없는.

Impossible to live without money,
having money yet still not living.

744

진실로 소중한 것들은
잃어보지 않고는 귀한 줄 모른다.

Unless you loose them,
we do not realize
the value of truly precious things.

지상의 사람은 누구나 단 한 뼘이라도
자기만의 정원을 가져야 한다네.

Every person in the world
should have their own garden,
no matter how small.

믿음은 모든 일의 근본이다.
믿음이 흔들리면 모든 것이 무너진다.

Trust is the basis of everything.
If trust is shaken, everything falls.

거짓은 유통기한이 있다.
자, 이제 진실의 시간이다.

Lies have an expiration date.
Now it's truth's turn.

내일이면 모두가 웃으며 오실 길을
오늘 젖은 얼굴로 걸어가는 사람아.

You walk today with
a tearful face along the path
down which tomorrow all
will come laughing.

나의 글이
배부른 자의 간식이 아닌
가난한 자의 양식이기를.

I would like my writing
to become food for the poor,
not a snack for the well-fed.

하얀 눈이 서리서리 쌓이는 날,
너는 나를 잊으라 잊어버리라.
하얗게 하얗게 잊어버리라.

On days when white snow coils deep,
you should forget me, forget me fully.
Forget me whitely, whitely.

고독은 깊은 고독만이 위로할 수 있다.
상처는 더 큰 상처만이 품어줄 수 있다.
슬픔은 더 큰 슬픔으로 흘러가야 한다.

Solitude can only
be comforted by deep solitude.
Only a greater wound
can embrace a wound.
Sorrow has to go flowing off
as a yet greater sorrow.

오늘은 오늘로 충분한 것.
오늘의 실망도 미움도 괴로움도 그만 접자.
새도 지친 날개를 접는다.
접어야 다시 내일의 창공을 날 수 있으니.

Today is sufficient for today.
Now let's fold up today's disappointment,
hatred and agony.
Birds fold weary wings, too.
They have to fold them
in order to fly through
tomorrow's blue skies again.

삶은 어디서나
저마다 최선을 다해 피어나는 꽃이다.

Anywhere, life for everyone
is a flower doing its very best to bloom.

뼈 아프고 고독할 때 감사하라.
내 사람이 크고 있는 것이니.

When in pain and lonesome,
give thanks.
Within you are great.

이대로 영영 눈보라 속으로 사라지거나
전혀 새로운 사람이 되어 돌아올 것만 같은
눈부신 흰 설원의 아침 길.

A dazzlingly white
early morning snow-covered path,
like vanishing completely into a blizzard
or coming back as someone made utterly new.

하루하루가 최초의 날이다.
하루하루가 위대한 선물이다.
참 좋은 날이다.

Each day is the first day.
Each day is a great gift.
What a wonderful day!

물은 세 걸음만 흘러도
스스로 맑아지듯
내 안에는 마르지 않고 흐르는
치유의 힘이 있다.

Just as water needs only to take
three steps to grow clear
there is a healing force
flowing ceaselessly within me.

영혼이 말하게 침묵하여라.
광야가 말하듯, 사막이 말하듯,
밤하늘의 별들이 말하듯,
영혼이 말하게 하여라.

Be silent so that the soul can speak.
As the wilderness speaks,
as the desert speaks,
as the stars in the night sky speak,
so let the soul speak.

인생의 고통은 끝이 없겠지요.
그 고통을 감내하고 이겨내는
인간의 능력 또한 끝이 없지요.

There seems to be
no end to life's pain.
Just as there is
no end to people's ability
to endure and overcome it.

나는 세상을 '위하여'
살기를 바라지 않는다.
진정한 나 자신을 살아가는 길이
세상을 위한 길이기를 바랄 뿐.

I do not hope to live 'for' the world.
I merely hope that the way
I live my true life
will be a way for the world.

가장 어려운 때가
도약의 지점이다.

The most difficult times
are the point of a new take-off.

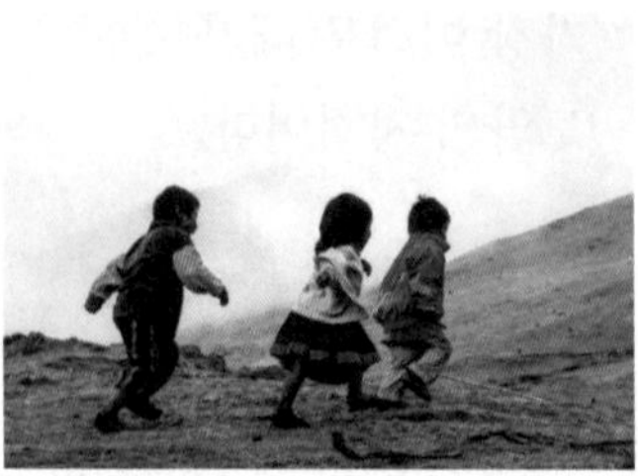

세상을 다 가졌어도 진정
사랑이 없고 우정이 없다면
인생은 아무것도, 아무것도 아니다.

Even if owning the whole world, truly
without love, without friendship,
human life is nothing, nothing.

아무도 밟지 않은 설원에
아침 발자국을 새기듯
책 속의 흰 눈길을
검은 눈동자로 사락사락 걷네.

Like morning footprints
inscribed on untrodden snow,
I go crunching across
a book's white path
with my dark eyes.

나이가 드니 날이 참 길군요.
나이가 드니 날이 참 짧군요.

As I grow older,
how long the days are!
As I grow older,
how short the days are!

꽃이 지는 건 꽃의 완주이듯
죽음은 삶의 완성일 뿐.
삶의 반대는 죽음이 아니다.
삶의 반대는 다 살지 못함이다.

Just as a flower's wilting
is the end of the flower,
death is merely
the completion of life.
The opposite of life
is not death.
The opposite of life
is not having lived fully.

나는 나에게 가장 먼 자가 되어버렸다.
나는 나에게 가장 낯선 자가 되어버렸다.

I have become the person
farthest from myself.
I have become the person
most unfamiliar to me.

어디서도 회의가 구름처럼 일어나고
무얼 해도 불안이 안개처럼 서성일 때,
사람들 속에서 나를 잃는 것만 같을 때,
침묵과 고독의 성소를 찾을 일이다.

Wherever doubts arise like clouds
and when anxiety hovers like mist,
no matter what I do,
when I feel lost among other people,
it is time to seek the sanctuary
of silence and solitude.

무릎 꿇는 힘으로
다시 일어서기 위하여.

Ever ready to stand up again
with the strength with which
I fell to my knees.

키 큰 나무 숲을 지나니 내 키가 커졌다.
깊은 강물을 건너니 내 영혼이 깊어졌다.

As I walked between tall trees, I grew taller.
As I crossed a deep river, my soul grew deeper.

오직 인간만이
더 나아지기를 바라는 존재다.
희망은, 인간의 영원한 불치병이다.

We humans are the only creatures
that aspire to grow better.
Hope is our everlasting, incurable disease.

798

사랑은 내가 가진
가장 소중한 것을 내어주는 것.
난 가진 것이 목숨뿐이기에
하루하루 목숨 바쳐 사랑했으니.

Loving is giving away
the most precious thing I have.
Since life is all I have
I have given my life loving you
day by day.

적은 소유로 기품 있게.

Gracefully
with few possessions.

아이가 태어나면
아이와 함께 자랄
나무 한 그루 심어요.
기쁠 땐 안고 웃고
슬플 땐 기대 우는
나무 한 그루 심어요.

Whenever a child is born
we plant a tree
that will grow up with it,
we plant a tree
for it to hug and laugh
on joyful days,
to lean against
and cry on sad days.

나의 기도는
반드시 이루어져 왔다.
기도 중에 헛된 바람은
다 사라져 버렸기에.

My prayer was surely granted.
Having rid myself
of all false hopes while praying.

희망希望은
희박하고 희미하여
희망인 것이다.

Hope
is slight and faint
and therefore hope.

처음부터 패배를 각오한 자에게
패배는 그 자체로 미래의 승리다.

For anyone prepared for defeat
from the start,
that defeat itself is future victory.

한 해를 돌아보며
나에게 선물로 다가온
올해의 귀인은 누구였던가.
나를 남김없이 불사른
올해의 시간은 언제였던가.

Looking back over the year gone by,
who was the special person
who came to me as a gift?
What moment this year
burned me up completely?

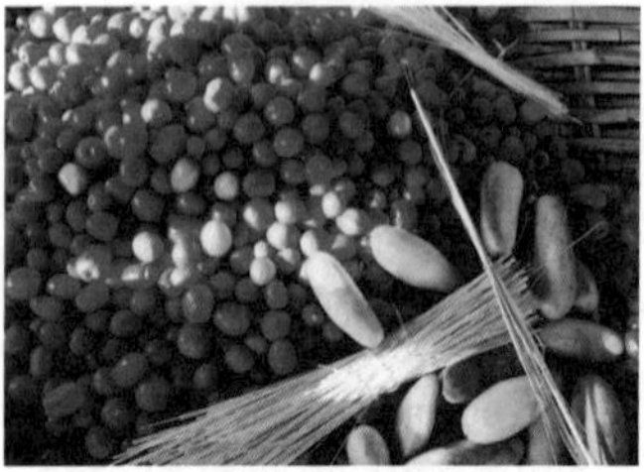

베푼 것은 잊고
받은 것은 기억하기.

Forgetting
what was given away,
recalling
what was received.

인간의 행복과 불행은 다 관계에서 오는 것.
관계만 튼튼하면 우리는 살 수 있다.

Human happiness and unhappiness
all come from relationships.
If the relationships are strong, we can live.

진리를 알려고 하는가
진리를 살려고 하는가.
사랑을 가지려 하는가
사랑을 하려고 하는가.

Are you trying to know the truth?
Are you trying to live the truth?
Are you trying to possess love?
Are you trying to love?

내 작은 글씨가
꽃씨였으면 좋겠다.
네 가슴에 심겨지는.

I wish my little letters
were flower seeds
sown in your heart.

너무 힘들어 난 여기까지인가
그만 등 돌리고 싶을 때,
힘든 게 아니라 간절하지 않은 것이다.

When I feel that's enough, it's too hard,
and want to turn back,
it's not that it's hard,
it's that I'm not in earnest.

얼음장 아래로 흐르는 물이 해맑듯
어려움이 많은 마음일수록
더 푸른 봄물로 흘러가리라.

Just as the water flowing under ice is pure,
the more difficulties the heart has
the more it will flow as blue spring water.

824

주지 않는 사랑은
지고 나르는 고통이다.

The love that you do not give
is the pain that you carry.

우리 일은
세상의 빛을 보기보다
내 안의 빛을 찾는 것.
우리 삶은
사람을 상대하기보다
하늘을 상대로 하는 것.

Rather than
seeing the world's light,
our task is to seek
for the light within myself.
Rather than
dealing with people,
our lives are a matter
of dealing with heaven.

마음아 천천히
천천히 걸어라.
내 영혼이 길을 잃지 않도록.

Ah, heart, slowly,
slowly, walk.
Lest my soul lose its way.

슬픔에도 기쁨에도 끝이 있다.
사랑에도 이별에도 끝이 있다.
끝이 있기에 둥근 시작이다.

Both sorrow and joy have an ending.
Both love and parting have an ending.
Since there's an end,
there's a smooth beginning.

사랑하는 사람아
우리에게 겨울이 없다면
무엇으로 따뜻한 포옹이 가능하겠느냐.
무엇으로 우리 서로 깊어질 수 있겠느냐.

Ah, you who love!
If we did not have winter,
how would a warm embrace be possible?
How would we each grow deeper together?

가지면 가질수록
가진 것에 마음을 두게 되었다.
비우면 비울수록
내 그리운 것에 마음을 두게 되었다.

The more I had,
the more I grew attached
to what I had.
The emptier I grew,
the more I grew attached
to what I longed for.

처음 해보는 부모 노릇,
처음 해보는 아이 노릇,
모자라고 실수투성이인 우리가 만나
서로 가르치고 격려하고 채워주며
언젠가 이별이 오는 그날까지
이 지상에서 한 생을 동행하기를.

Being parents for the first time,
being a child for the first time,
we meet, all of us falling short,
a mass of mistakes,
teach, encourage, add to each other
until the day comes when we part,
accompanying a life in this world.

오늘은 사랑 하나로 충분한 날.
우리 오늘처럼만 사랑하자.

Today is a day satisfied by a single love.
Let's just love like today.

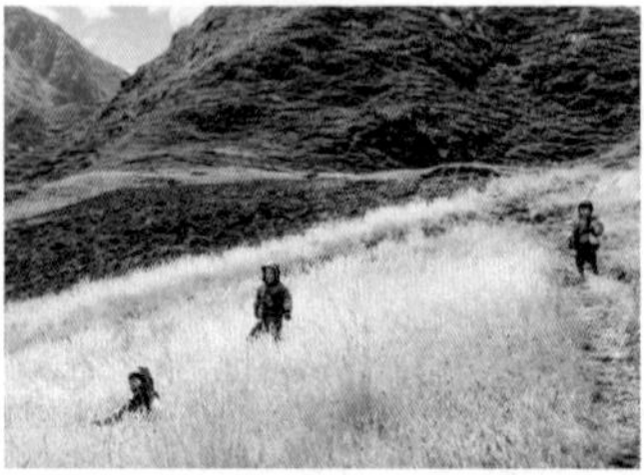

그만 배우기, 깨쳐내기.
그만 말하기, 살아내기.

No more learning, mastering.
No more talking, managing.

12월에는 등 뒤를 돌아보자.
내 그립고 눈물 나는 것들은 다
등 뒤에서 서성이고 있으니.
앞만 보고 달려온 시간에
고요히 등 뒤를 돌아보자.

In December, let's look back.
All the things I longed for and wept over
are walking along behind me.
At times when we have
gone rushing on, only looking ahead,
let's quietly look back.

좋은 날은 짧았고
힘든 날은 많았다.
그래도 우리는 살아왔다.
그래도 삶은 나아간다.

Good days were short,
hard days were many.
Yet still we went living on.
Yet still life goes on.

지금까지 본 별들은
수억 광년 전에 출발한 빛.
가장 빛나는 별은 지금
간절하게 길을 찾는 너에게로
빛의 속도로 달려오고 있으니.

The stars you have seen hitherto
are rays of light
that set out billions of light years ago.
The brightest star is even now
hastening toward you
at the speed of light
as you desperately seek a path.

'이름'이란 나를 '일러'내는 것.
내가 이르러야만 할 생의 길에
가만히 내 이름을 불러본다.

My 'name' is how I am 'named.'
Along the way to the life
I must attain
I silently call my name.

좋은 마침이 있어야
새로운 시작이 있다.

There have to be
good endings
for there to be
new beginnings.

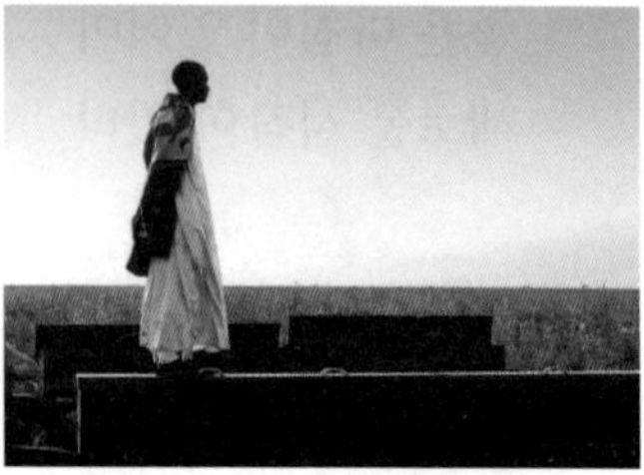

긴 호흡
강한 걸음.

Deep breathing.
Strong walking.

안 되면 안 한다.
되는 대로 한다.
될 일은 반드시 될 것이다.

I do not do what I cannot do.
I do what I can do.
What can be done will surely be done.

오늘도 길을 걷는 우리는
알 수 없는 먼 곳에서 와서
알 수 없는 그곳으로 돌아간다.
우리의 힘든 발자국들은
한 줌 이슬처럼 바람에 흩어지니.
그러나 염려하지 마라.
그 고독한 길을 지금
우리 함께 걷고 있으니.

As we walk along today,
leaving an unknown place
we return to that unknown place.
Our plodding steps
scatter like dewdrops in the wind.
But don't worry.
We are walking together
along those lonesome paths.

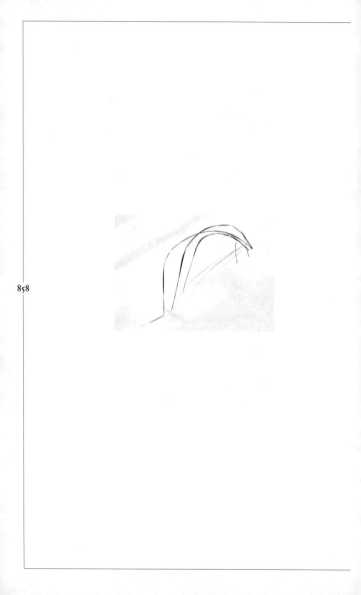

좋은 것들은 남겨두기를.
하늘만이 아는 일도
하늘만이 하실 일도
여백처럼 남겨두기를.

Leave good things.
Leave what Heaven alone knows,
what Heaven alone will do,
like blank spaces.

사랑하다 죽는 것은 두려운 일이지만
사랑 없이 사는 것은 더 두려운 일이다.
사랑은 죽음보다 강하다.

To die of love is a fearful thing
but to live without love
is even more fearful.
Love is stronger than death.

겨울바람이 언 가슴을 울리면
오, 봄이 멀지 않으리.

When winter winds
make the breast resound,
ah, spring cannot be far off.

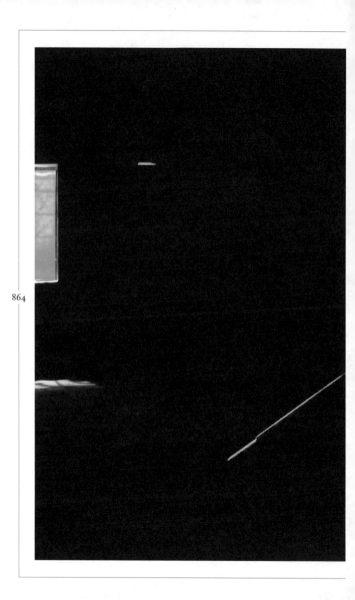

나는 단 한 권의 책을 써 나가고 있다.
삶이라는 단 한 권의 책을.
생을 다 바쳐 쓴 내 소멸의 책을.

I am engaged in writing just one book,
a single volume entitled Life,
my expiring book written with all my life.

서둘지 마라. 그러나 쉬지도 마라.
위대한 것은 다 자신만의 때가 있으니.

Don't hurry but never rest.
Everything great has its own time.

마음이 사무치면 꽃이 핀다.

When the heart is touched,
flowers bloom.

박노해
Park Nohae

글·사진 **박노해**

1957 전라남도에서 태어났다. 16세에 상경해 노동자로 일하며 선린상고(야간)를 다녔다. **1984** 스물일곱 살에 첫 시집 『노동의 새벽』을 펴냈다. 이 시집은 군사독재 정권의 금서 조치에도 100만 부가 발간되며 한국 사회와 문단을 충격으로 뒤흔들었다. 감시를 피해 사용한 박노해라는 필명은 '박해받는 노동자 해방'이라는 뜻으로, 이때부터 '얼굴 없는 시인'으로 불렸다. **1989** 〈남한사회주의노동자동맹〉(사노맹)을 결성했다.

1991 7년여의 수배 끝에 안기부에 체포, 24일간의 고문 후 '반국가단체 수괴' 죄목으로 사형이 구형되고 무기징역에 처해졌다. **1993** 감옥 독방에서 두 번째 시집 『참된 시작』을 펴냈다. **1997** 옥중에세이 『사람만이 희망이다』를 펴냈다. **1998** 7년 6개월의 수감 끝에 석방됐다. 이후 민주화운동가로 복권됐으나 국가보상금을 거부했다. **2000** "과거를 팔아 오늘을 살지 않겠다"며 권력의 길을 뒤로 하고 비영리단체 〈나눔문화〉(www.nanum.com)를 설립했다. **2003** 이라크 전쟁터에 뛰어들면서, 세계의 가난과 분쟁 현장에서 평화활동을 이어왔다. **2010** 낡은 흑백 필름 카메라로 기록

한 사진을 모아 첫 사진전 「라 광야」展과 「나 거기에 그들처럼」展(세종문화회관)을 열었다. 12년 만의 시집 『그러니 그대 사라지지 말아라』를 펴냈다. 2012 나눔문화가 운영하는 〈라 카페 갤러리〉에서 박노해 사진전을 상설 개최하고 있다. 현재 22번째 전시를 이어가고 있으며, 총 39만 명의 관람객이 다녀갔다. 2014 아시아 사진전 「다른 길」展(세종문화회관) 개최와 함께 사진집 『다른 길』을 펴냈다. 2019 박노해 사진에세이 시리즈 『하루』를 시작으로 『단순하게 단단하게 단아하게』, 『길』, 『내 작은 방』, 『아이들은 놀라워라』, 『올리브 나무 아래』를 펴냈다. 2020 시 그림책 『푸른 빛의 소녀가』, 2021 『걷는 독서』, 2022 시집 『너의 하늘을 보아』, 2024 첫 자전수필 『눈물꽃 소년』을 펴냈다. 30여 년간 써온 책, 우주에서의 인간의 길을 담은 사상서를 집필 중이다. '적은 소유로 기품 있게' 살아가는 〈참사람의 숲〉을 꿈꾸며, 시인의 작은 정원에서 꽃과 나무를 심고 기르며 새로운 혁명의 길로 나아가고 있다.

박노해의 걷는 독서　🅕 parknohae　🅞 park_nohae

Park Nohae is a legendary poet, photographer and revolutionary. He was born in 1957. While working as a laborer in his 20s, he began to reflect and write poems on the sufferings of the laboring class. He then took the pseudonym Park Nohae ("No" means "laborers," "Hae" means "liberation"). At the age of twenty-seven, Park published his first collection of poems, titled *The Dawn of Labor*, in 1984. Despite official bans, this collection sold nearly a million copies, and it shook Korean society with its shocking emotional power. Since then, he became an intensely symbolic figure of resistance, often called the "Faceless Poet." For several years the government authorities tried to arrest him in vain. He was finally arrested in 1991. After twenty-four days of investigation, with illegal torture, the death penalty was demanded for his radical ideology. He was finally sentenced to life imprisonment. After seven and a half years in prison, he was pardoned in 1998. Thereafter, he was reinstated as a contributor to the democratization movement, but he refused any state compensation. Park decided to leave the way for power, saying, "I will not live today by selling the past," and he established a nonprofit social movement organization "Nanum Munhwa," meaning "Culture of Sharing," (www.nanum.com) faced with the great challenges confronting global humanity. In 2003, right after the United States' invasion of Iraq, he flew to the field of war. Since then, he often visits countries that are suffering from war and poverty, such as Iraq, Palestine, Pakistan, Sudan, Tibet and Banda Aceh, in order to raise awareness about the situation through his photos and writings. He continues to hold photo exhibitions, and a total of 390,000 visitors have so far visited his exhibitions. He is writing a book of reflexions, the only such book he has written during the thirty years since prison, "The Human Path in Space." Dreaming of the Forest of True People, a life-community living "a graceful life with few possessions," the poet is still planting and growing flowers and trees in his small garden, advancing along the path toward a new revolution.

Reading While Walking Along ⓕ parknohae ⓞ park_nohae

저서

눈물꽃 소년 박노해 자전수필

박노해 시인의 소년시대 성장기. 곱고 정감 어린 사투리와 시인이 직접 그린 연필 그림이 더해져, 그가 자란 어린 날이 영화처럼 펼쳐진다. 어떻게 강인하고 사랑 많은 어른으로 자랄 수 있었는지 그 원형이 담긴 33편의 이야기. 할머니와 어머니, 마을 어른들과 선생님, 친구들과 첫사랑의 소녀까지, 울고 웃다 보면 영혼의 키가 훌쩍 자라날 책. 256p | 18,000 | 2024

너의 하늘을 보아 박노해 시집

무언가 잘못된 세상에 절망할 때, 하루하루 내 존재가 희미해져갈 때, 빛과 힘이 되어줄 301편의 시. 고난과 어둠 속에서도 '빛을 찾아가는 여정'에 자신을 두었던 박노해 시인의 투혼과 사랑의 삶이 전하는 울림. 그 시를 읽기 전의 나로 돌아갈 수 없는 강렬한 체험. "아무것도 없다고 생각되는 순간조차, 우리에게는 자신만의 하늘이 있다." 528p | 19,500 | 2022

박노해 사진에세이 시리즈 01 하루 02 단순하게 단단하게 단아하게 03 길 04 내 작은 방 05 아이들은 놀라워라 06 올리브나무 아래 20여 년 동안 지상의 멀고 높은 길을 걸으며 기록해온 유랑노트이자 길 찾는 이에게 띄우는 두꺼운 편지. 각 권마다 37점의 흑백사진과 캡션이 담겼다. 인생이란 한 편의 이야기이며 '에세이'란 그 이야기를 남겨놓는 것이니. 삶의 화두와도 같은 주제로 매년 새 시리즈가 출간된다. 128p | 20,000 | 2019-2023

그러니 그대 사라지지 말아라 박노해 시집

영혼을 뒤흔드는 시의 정수. 저항과 영성, 교육과 살림, 아름다움과 혁명 그리고 사랑까지, 표지만큼이나 붉은 304편의 시가 담겼다. 인생의 갈림길에서 길을 잃고 헤매는 순간마다 어디를 펼쳐 봐도 좋을 책. 입소문만으로 이 시집을 구입한 7만 명의 독자가 증명하는 감동. "그러니 그대 사라지지 말아라" 그 한 마디가 나를 다시 살게 한다. 560p | 18,000 | 2010

노동의 새벽 박노해 첫 시집

1984년, 27살의 '얼굴 없는 시인'이 쓴 시집 한 권이 세상을 뒤흔들었다. 독재정부의 금서 조치에도 100만 부가 발간되며 화인처럼 새겨진 불멸의 고전. 억압받는 천만 노동자의 영혼의 북소리로 울려퍼진 노래. "박노해는 역사이고 상징이며 신화다. 문학사적으로나 사회적으로 우리는 그런 존재를 다시 만날 수 없을지 모른다."(문학평론가 도정일) 172p | 12,000 | 2014

사람만이 희망이다 박노해 옥중에세이

34살의 나이에 '불온한 혁명가'로 무기징역을 선고받은 박노해. 그가 1평 남짓한 감옥 독방에 갇혀 7년여 동안 침묵 정진 속에 써내려간 옥중에세이. "90년대 최고의 정신적 각성"으로 기록되는 이 책은, 희망이 보이지 않는 오늘날 더 큰 울림으로 되살아난다. 살아있는 한 희망은 끝나지 않았다고. 다시, 사람만이 희망이라고. 320p | 15,000 | 2015

Books

The Tear-Flowering Boy Childhood Stories

The story of poet Park Nohae's childhood. With beautiful and affectionate regional dialect and pencil drawings by the poet himself, the childhood days he grew up unfold like a movie. 33 stories relating how he grew up to be a strong and loving adult. This is a book that will make your soul grow taller as you cry and laugh with his grandmother, mother, village elders, teachers, friends, and even his first love. 256p | 18,000KRW | 2024

Seeing Your Heaven Collection of Poems

301 poems that will give you light and strength when you despair in a world gone wrong, when your soul seems to be fading away day by day. The reverberations of the life of love and fighting spirit of poet Park Nohae, who set out on a 'journey in search of light' in the midst of hardship and darkness. An intense experience that makes it impossible to return to who I was before I read the poems. "Even when we think there is nothing, we each have our own heaven." 528p | 19,500KRW | 2022

Park Nohae Photo Essay

01 One Day 02 Simply, Firmly, Gracefully 03 The Path 04 My Dear Little Room 05 Children Are Amazing 06 Beneath The Olive Trees

These are 'wandering notes' that the poet Park Nohae has recorded while walking along the Earth's long, high roads for over twenty years, a thick letter to those who seek for a path. Each volume contains 37 black-and-white photos and captions. Life is a story, and each of these 'essays' is designed to leave that story behind. A new volume is published every year like a topic of life. 128p | 20,000KRW | 2019-2023

So You Must Not Disappear Collection of Poems

The essence of soul-shaking poetry! This anthology of 304 poems as red as its book cover, narrating resistance, spirituality, education, living, the beautiful, revolution and love. Whenever you're lost at a cross-roads of your life, it will guide you with any page of it moving you. The intensity of moving is evidenced by the 70,000 readers who have bought this book only through word-of-mouth. "So you must not disappear." This one phrase makes me live again. 560p | 18,000KRW | 2010

The Dawn of Labor Collection of Poems

In 1984, an anthology of poems written by 27 years old "faceless poet" shook Korean society. Recorded as a million seller despite the publication ban under military dictatorship, it became an immortal classic ingrained like a marking iron. It was a song echoing down with the throbbing pulses of ten million workers' souls. "Park Nohae is a history, a symbol, and a myth. All the way through the history of literature and society alike, we may never meet such a being again."(Doh Jeong-il, literary critic) 172p | 12,000KRW | 2014

Only a Person is Hope Essay Written in Prison

Park Nohae was sentenced to life imprisonment as a "rebellious revolutionary" when 34 years old. This essay written in solitary confinement measuring about three sq. m. for seven years. This book is recorded as the "best spiritual awakening in the 90s," is born again with the bigger impression today when there seems to be no hope at all. As long as you live, hope never ends. Again, only a person is hope. 320p | 15,000KRW | 2015

걷는 독서

3판 32쇄 발행 2024년 11월 26일
초판 1쇄 발행 2021년 6월 7일

글·사진 박노해
번역 안선재 디자인 홍동원 편집 김예슬, 윤지영 제작 윤지혜 홍보 이상훈
인쇄 천광인쇄사 제본 광성문화사 후가공 신화사금박, 이지앤비
발행인 임소희 발행처 느린걸음 출판등록 2002.3.15 제300-2009-109호
주소 서울시 종로구 사직로8길 34, 330호 instagram @slow_walk_book

Reading While Walking Along

Third edition, 32th publishing, Nov. 26, 2024
First edition, first publishing, Jun. 7, 2021

Texts and photos by Park Nohae
Translation by Brother Anthony of Taizé
Designed by Hong Dongwon Edited by Kim Yeseul, Yun Jiyoung
Making by Yun Jihye Marketing by Lee Sanghoon Publisher Im Sohee
Publishing Company Slow Walking instagram @slow_walk_book
Address Rm330, 34, Sajik-ro 8-gil, Jongno-gu, Seoul, Republic of Korea